"One of the mo...

Sunday Times

Twice winner of the Hugo Award, Bob Shaw is one of Britain's most popular science-fiction writers. Born in Belfast, where he worked as a journalist, he now lives in Warrington, Cheshire, and has three grown-up children. His principal hobbies are making stained-glass lampshades, metal detecting and real ale. He is a well-known speaker at science-fiction conventions, at which he has been guest of honour many times, in countries including UK, USA, France, Italy, Poland, Denmark, Australia and New Zealand.

Bob Shaw is the author of numerous short stories and over twenty novels, including *The Ragged Astronauts*. *Killer Planet* is his first book for young people.

KILLER PLANET

Bob Shaw

PAN PIPER
PAN MACMILLAN
CHILDREN'S BOOKS

First published 1989 by Victor Gollancz Ltd

This Pan Piper edition published 1992 by
Pan Macmillan Children's Books Ltd
a division of Pan Macmillan Publishers Limited
Cavaye Place London SW10 9PG
and Basingstoke

Associated companies throughout the world

ISBN 0 330 31696 6

1 3 5 7 9 8 6 4 2

A CIP catalogue record for this book is available from
the British Library

Typeset by Rowland Phototypesetting Ltd, Bury St Edmunds
Printed and bound in Great Britain by
Cox & Wyman Ltd, Reading, Berkshire

Prologue

The year is 2194 AD and it is now more than two centuries since men and women took their first hesitant steps into the vastness of space.

At first there were the tiny hops to the Moon, accomplished in ridiculously flimsy metal shells; then with advancing technology came the manned flights to Mars. Soon afterwards the invention of the Gemmell drive enabled the great spaceships from Earth to leap instantaneously from star to star. And now, suddenly, human beings are embarking on the ultimate adventure—the exploration of the galaxy.

Inevitably, there are awesome dangers.

In addition to the risks of space flight itself, there are myriads of deadly alien life forms to contest the ownership of each newly discovered world. It is as though Nature has set out to test her ingenuity at devising strange and terrible ways for brave men and women to die; as though this is the price they have to pay for daring to pit themselves against the immensities of the universe.

And, of all the implacable foes that space travellers have encountered thus far, the most mysterious—the most *deadly*—is undoubtedly the Killer Planet.

Discovered in 2191 AD and officially named Verdia, the Killer Planet prowls its elliptical path around a yellow G-type sun. Its entire surface is shrouded by dense vapours which cannot be penetrated by orbiting cameras. Those vapours preserve the mystery of how hundreds of brave men and women met their deaths on Verdia within hours of landing. Although no surface features are visible from space, the shield of cloud glows intermittently as electrical storms rage from pole to pole, evidence of the incredible bolts of energy being unleashed in the tortured atmosphere.

More than two years have passed since the Killer Planet claimed its last victims—and now it is hungry again.

Hungry, watchful, waiting . . .

Chapter 1

It was a fine summer morning and the air above the concrete expanse of the Jacksonville Commercial Spacefield was already beginning to shimmer in the growing heat. The hangars, workshops and office buildings of the various transport companies which used the field as their head-quarters gleamed in the strong Florida sunlight. A faint breeze wafting in from the Atlantic sent swirls of dust dancing across the flat ground, but failed to bring any coolness to the interiors of the big warp-drive freighters whose towering hulls dominated the scene. Mechanical handling vehicles bustled continuously among the starships, loading or unloading interstellar cargoes, their drivers occasionally dabbing sweat from their faces and thinking wist-fully about the next refreshment break.

In contrast to the noise and activity outside, the scene inside the office of the Hazard Line was quiet and almost religiously solemn. Donn Hazard, owner of the shipping line, had just opened a bottle of champagne and was pouring the sparkling liquid into four plastic cups. Donn was a tall man with friendly but commanding features, and although he was nearing fifty his black hair was only slightly flecked with grey. He smiled as he finished pouring the champagne and handed a cup to each of the three much younger people who were standing by his desk.

"This is my last bottle of bubbly—it's just too expensive

these days—but it's the most fitting drink for a celebration," he said. "I want to show my appreciation for all the hard work you've done in the last year. Without your help the *Seeker* would never have been finished—so here's to the successful conclusion of the most important project of my life!"

He turned and raised his cup towards the sleek crimson shape of the *Seeker*, which was visible through the office window. The specially designed rocket ship was only fifteen metres from needle prow to tail, a symphony of streamlined curvatures, and was sitting vertically upright on a multi-wheeled transporter at the edge of the spacefield.

Jan Hazard, Donn's son, echoed the toast and sipped dutifully from his cup, hiding the fact that the dry wine was unpleasantly bitter to his taste. Already as tall as his father, Jan had thick black hair and the muscular frame of a natural athlete. His features were pleasantly unremarkable, but at times his face bore a look of seriousness which made him seem older than his sixteen years. He and his two best friends—Petra Moir and Ozburt Groom—had been devoting every minute they could spare from their education schedules to the *Seeker* project and were justifiably proud of the outcome. Jan felt a great sense of personal achievement on seeing the little ship completed, but his pleasure was tempered by deep concern about what was supposed to happen next.

His father was absolutely determined to fly the *Seeker* single-handedly down through the eternal cloud cover of the planet Verdia. It was bad enough that nobody who had landed on Verdia had ever come back, but Jan had an even greater cause to worry about his father's safety.

So intense were his fears that he had recently come to the

4

most momentous decision of his life, one which had to be kept secret at all costs.

"My nose!" Ozburt snorted, choking over his drink. "It's hurting my nose! Do people actually enjoy drinking this stuff?" He was a chubby-faced redhead who had great difficulty in controlling his outsized hands and feet, but behind his clumsiness was a rare talent for all forms of electronic engineering. It was his seemingly instinctive skill in maintaining the flight simulator which had made it possible for Donn to practise 'flying' the *Seeker*, even though the unique ship had never left the ground.

"We grown-ups enjoy champagne," Petra told him cool-ly. "You should stick to your cherry sodas." She was tall and athletic looking, with fair hair and tanned skin which had earned her the apt nickname of the Golden Girl of the school sports squad. Her favourite sport was archery, in which she had won several junior championships. Jan often thought it ironic that it was prowess in such an ancient sport which had enabled her to play an important role in his father's preparations for the mission to Verdia. In the strange conditions of that planet modern weapons were worse than useless, and for self-defence his father planned to rely largely on a bow and arrows. Petra had devoted a lot of time to teaching him to shoot accurately.

"Grown-ups! Listen to old Granny Moir!" Ozburt replied. "You're only five months older than I am."

"That's going by the calendar, but if you consider *mental* age I'm . . ."

"That's enough of that, you two," Donn put in. "Remember we're all part of a team. Isn't that right, Jan?"

"I agree," Jan said, meeting his father's gaze squarely.

5

"And that's why I think I should be going to Verdia with you—as part of a team."

"We've already been through all that, and my decision is final." Donn set his cup down, signalling that the impromptu celebration was over. "This is a job for me alone."

"But . . ."

"For me *alone*, Jan." For a moment the expression in Donn's eyes was troubled as he gazed at his son, then he produced a smile for the benefit of all three young people. "Now, if the gang will kindly get out of here I'll be able to get on with some urgent work. There are quite a lot of last-minute details to take care of if I'm going to take off tomorrow morning."

"We have things to do as well," Petra said tactfully. "We'll see you later." She set her cup aside, gestured for Jan and Ozburt to do likewise, and ushered the two out of the office.

"Don't shove!" Ozburt's round face looked indignant as they emerged to the fierce sunlight of the spacefield. "What's the mother hen routine for? Huh?"

"Mr Hazard has enough on his mind without you cluttering up his office." Petra turned to Jan. "And I don't think you should keep on arguing with him."

"Don't you?" Jan said heatedly. "Perhaps you'd think differently if it was *your* brother that was missing and presumed dead."

Before she could reply he spun on his heel and strode away in the direction of the transporter upon which waited the crimson shape of the *Seeker*, the unique spaceship built to his father's own design. As he neared the huge vehicle and its load his thoughts returned to the enigma of the planet called Verdia, the distant and mysterious world which had claimed his only brother . . .

Although Verdia's surface was totally obscured by cloud, the exploration ship which discovered the planet in 2191 was able to gather a substantial amount of information by conducting radar soundings and an instrument survey from orbit. Verdia was covered by a warm green ocean, except for one large land mass at the northern pole, where there were extensive deposits of valuable minerals. The single continent lay under a continuous blanket of dense jungle which probably harboured many species of alien wildlife.

In short, Verdia was far from being an ideal planet for colonisation, but Earth was already becoming expert in terraforming—that branch of engineering which dealt with modifying conditions on new worlds to make them more suitable for human habitation. Earth's own Moon and the desert planet of Mars had been the first examples, their hostile environments altered by such means as importing water in the form of ice asteroids. It was decided to proceed with the occupation of Verdia, and a development team was sent in to prepare the planet for the arrival of settlers.

But what had started off as a routine operation soon went disastrously wrong.

Shortly after landing the engineers radioed back reports of finding the overgrown ruins of an ancient city—then all communication abruptly ceased.

The covering of cloud prevented any optical study of the situation from orbit, so a robot survey module was sent down to gather data. The torpedo-shaped module darted down through the clouds and skimmed low over the engineers' landing site. It had time to send back grim pictures which showed dead bodies lying among wrecked and abandoned equipment—then it went out of control and crashed.

The next step was that a heavily armed and well-equipped trouble-shooting team from the Stellar Expeditionary Force was dispatched to the surface to investigate. They managed to send back a few seconds of garbled reports about their vehicles, machinery and weapons 'going wild', then they too fell silent.

A second survey module established that they had met a fate similar to that of the engineers, but its transmissions were cut short when it also went out of control and plunged to the ground.

Scientists who were observing from spacecraft in orbit noticed that at the exact time of each disaster there were severe disturbances in the planet's powerful magnetic field. The most obvious sign had been the flurries of lightning which had danced around the landing sites. A theory was put forward that any large metallic object—such as a bulldozer or a tank—reaching the surface of Verdia attracted lightning bursts which destroyed the machines and killed their operators.

Unsubstantiated though the theory was, it was accepted by the politicians who made up the Council of Empire. A planet where machines could not be used was of no value, and other less troublesome worlds were waiting to be exploited. After a brief emergency session the Council declared Verdia a 'no-go' world and the official files on it were closed.

Jan Hazard, then a boy of thirteen, had heard the

Council's decision with shock and astonishment—because his older brother, Bari, had been with the Stellar Expeditionary Force.

It had been officially assumed—without proof—that there were no survivors of the Verdia mission, but every instinct that Jan possessed told him otherwise. Bari was tough, clever and resourceful, well-schooled in outdoor survival techniques, and an inner voice told Jan that he simply could not have died, no matter how hellish the scenes depicted in the reconnaissance photographs.

His father had thought along the same lines and had reacted with characteristic vigour and determination. Jan could remember his father—grim-faced and dark-eyed with exhaustion—fighting a months-long battle to have the Council's decision reversed, and only gradually coming to accept bitter defeat.

In all the history of exploration—from the taming of the Earth's continents to the conquest of space—mankind had never chosen to abandon an outpost. But now, simply because there was no commercial advantage in doing otherwise, the fat bureaucrats of the Council wanted to forget the brave men and women who had given their lives on Verdia. The planet was a 'bad investment risk'.

Jan could also recall his father's anger turning into a brooding, diamond-hard determination that no matter what the cost, no matter what dangers had to be faced, he was going to penetrate Verdia's stormy grey atmosphere and bring back his first son. The *Seeker*—a spaceship unlike any other—had been born out of that determination, and the time for it to be pitted against the mysteries and terrors of the Killer Planet had almost arrived.

As he walked across the scorched concrete of the spacefield, his gazed locked on the glowing red outline of the rocket ship, Jan felt a stirring of excitement underlaid with fear. He was in full accord with the objective of finding and rescuing Bari, and he had every confidence in the *Seeker*'s computer-assisted design—but there was one aspect of the plan which from the start had filled him with apprehension.

He was convinced that his father was the wrong person to pilot the *Seeker*, and that his insistence on tackling the mission single-handed would lead to yet another tragedy.

Donn had spent most of his early life as a flier and he was still fit, but he would soon be fifty and his reactions had slowed. That would not have mattered had he been proposing to use an ordinary ship, in which most of the pilot's work was handled by computers, but the *Seeker* had no automation whatsoever and flying it called for ultra-fast responses.

On a number of occasions the flight simulator had shown that Donn had been too late in making a vital control movement. Each time Donn had shrugged the matter off, claiming he would be fine on an actual flight, but Jan had known better and his apprehension had increased. Finally—and not without some feelings of guilt and disloyalty—he had reached a decision which he had confided to no other person.

When the time came to send the *Seeker* arrowing down towards the clouds of Verdia, no matter what last-minute trickery it took, he would be at the rocket ship's controls.

Alone!

Chapter 2

As the morning progressed the temperature at the Jackson-ville field had climbed steadily until exposed metal surfaces were too hot to touch. The work of maintaining and servicing the big starships went on as before, but the sounds of the cargo handling machines and repair robots now seemed to have a drowsy quality, as though even their metal limbs had been made sluggish by the oppressive heat. The air was heavy and humid, blurring the flat, distant horizon.

Jan was helping his father carry out final checks and adjustments on the controls of the *Seeker*. The time had almost arrived for the rocket ship to be moved out of the workshop area to the north side of the spacefield for loading on to the *Culcheth*, the specially adapted starship which would carry it across the light years to Verdia. Being small and chemically propelled, the *Seeker* was only capable of short-range orbital flight. To get it out of the Solar System and across the inconceivably vast distances that separate the stars, it was necessary for it to be carried in the cargo bay of the huge warp-driven freighter which could leap from one star to another in a fraction of a second.

The task of preparing the *Seeker* for flight involved frequently climbing from ground level up to the rocket ship's cockpit. Donn had been more than prepared to do his full share of the work, but Jan had seen him slowly becoming drained of energy by the punishing heat and had unobtrusively taken on the most demanding jobs. In spite of his superb physical condition he found himself sweating profusely from the exertion, a fact which strengthened his secret resolve about the Verdia mission.

Rescuing Bari from the Killer Planet was an undertaking for someone in his physical prime, and he would be able to afford no mistakes when the time came to take over from his father. He had not yet worked out exactly how he was going to do it—outwitting his father in such a matter would be far from easy—and his lack of a plan added to the uncertainties which clouded the near future. His feeling of urgency increased as he remembered how short was the time remaining to him. The *Seeker* was due to be taken aboard the *Culcheth* that very afternoon, and the warp jump to Verdia was scheduled for the following day . . .

"Jan, when are we going to break for lunch?" The voice from Jan's wrist communicator was that of Ozburt Groom, speaking from the control deck of the *Culcheth*, which was parked about a kilometre away. "I'm so hungry I could eat a Sirian lizard."

Jan leaned against one of the transporter's gigantic wheels and shook his head in disbelief. "You can't be hungry already."

"Don't forget I've had nothing since breakfast," Ozburt said plaintively. "That burger I had a couple of hours ago doesn't count—it was so small it's rattling around in my stomach."

"There's plenty of room for it," Jan replied, alluding to his friend's ample girth. "How's the work going over there?"

"Almost through—another hour or so will wrap it up."

"In that case wouldn't it be more sensible to finish off before you stop to feed your face?"

"Don't be such a slave-driver," Donn said, coming to stand by his side. "Ozburt is doing me a big favour by standing in for Ed."

He was referring to the fact that Ed Czubek, the Hazard Line's sole remaining freighter pilot, had taken a day's sick leave. Ozburt had volunteered in his place to carry out all the pre-flight checks on the *Culcheth* so that tomorrow's take-off would not be delayed.

"I'm sorry, Dad," Jan said, realising he had been unfair to Ozburt. "It's just that there's so little time left, and . . . and . . ."

"I know—the last two years have been a big strain on all of us." Donn squeezed his son's shoulder, demonstrating the affection he rarely put into words. "Now why don't you arrange to pick up Ozburt and Petra and I'll buy us all a lunch so big that even Ozburt will have to admit defeat?"

"Okay, Dad," Jan said, smiling. He was raising his communicator to his lips when he noticed two long grey cars bearing the county crest pulling up at the Hazard Line's office. A squat, soberly dressed man got out of the leading car, shading his eyes as he looked all about him, while Jan's father was approaching him. He had a hard and humourless face, and something in his manner made Jan feel strangely uneasy.

"Are you Donn Hazard?" the man said brusquely.

"I am." Donn showed some surprise. "What can I do for you?"

13

"You can take this." The stranger produced a folded document from one of his pockets. "It's a court order empowering me to impound all your assets pending bankruptcy proceedings against you."

"I . . ." Donn looked stunned, unable to comprehend what was happening. "What does this mean?"

"It means you haven't been paying your bills, Mr Hazard. It means you owe a lot of people a lot of money and they've gotten tired of waiting for it. My name is Weston, by the way, and—as you may have guessed—I'm a bailiff. I know the word has an old-fashioned ring to it these days, but a debt is still a debt."

"But this is ridiculous." Donn frowned as he opened the document. "There must have been a mistake. I know I've had to ask some people to wait a while, but . . ."

"It's been more than a while," Weston cut in. "Quite a few of your creditors have been waiting two years."

So it has finally happened, Jan thought, numbed with dismay. His father had been so obsessed with designing and building the *Seeker* and preparing for its desperate mission that everything else had ceased to have much meaning for him. Friends and colleagues had repeatedly warned him that his business was rapidly going downhill, but nothing had mattered to him other than the overwhelming need to build the ship which would rescue his son.

And the worst had finally come to pass—only hours before the take-off for Verdia.

"All right, I'll make you a deal," Donn said, forcing a smile with obvious effort as he pointed at the *Seeker*. "You can take everything except that."

Weston again shaded his eyes as he turned his attention to the smooth curvatures of the little ship which was poised on the transporter like a crimson bird ready to take flight.

"What in the name of . . . ?" His eyes widened with surprise. "That looks like a rocket ship!"

"That's exactly what it is."

"But why would anybody want a chemically powered ship in this day and age?"

"You could say it's an experimental vessel," Donn replied. "It was built to do one special job and it's of no value to anybody except me—so what do you say? Have we a deal?"

Weston shook his head. "I'm sorry. I'll have to impound everything, including that rocket—even if it's only for the scrap value."

"Scrap!" Jan was galvanised into stepping forward, his mind clamouring with anger and alarm. "You can't scrap the *Seeker*!"

Weston regarded him with unfriendly eyes. "I'm only doing my job, young man."

"Some job!" Jan said heatedly. "If you think you're just going to walk in here and . . ."

"It's all right, son," Donn cut in, then returned his attention to the bailiff. "Look, there's no need for all this rush is there? If you will come back in a couple of hours, I'll have my lawyer here and we can talk things over in a reasonable manner."

"No way!" Weston shook his head emphatically. "I go away for a couple of hours and come back to find that half your assets have mysteriously vanished. Nobody's going to pull that trick on me. No, sir!"

"I don't go in for trickery," Donn snapped, a gleam of anger in his eyes.

"I hope you're not thinking of trying anything foolish," Weston said, shifting uneasily. "I have quite a few men with me in case of trouble."

"Trouble?" Donn glanced past the stocky figure of the bailiff to where half-a-dozen men were getting out of the official cars and a look of resignation appeared on his face, making him look very tired. "I don't want trouble."

"I'm glad you feel that way," Weston said.

Jan was aghast as he listened. It came to him that two years of unremitting effort and worry had taken a terrible toll of his father's spirit. The monstrous unfairness of having the *Seeker* impounded on the very eve of its departure must have been the last straw for him. Jan clenched his fists as a tide of fury washed through his being. Was this going to be the futile end to all their hopes? Was his brother going to be condemned to eke out the rest of his life in the jungles of Verdia because of one petty official? *Never!*

Jan relaxed his fists and forced himself to look calm as a desperate plan began to form in his mind.

"Let's get it over and done with," Weston said, consulting a computer print-out. "Now, I understand you have a cargo ship called *Culcheth* at this field. Where is it?"

"Over there." Donn pointed out the rust-streaked hull of the *Culcheth*, which rose like a metallic steeple out of the heat haze a kilometre away.

A look of disdain spread across Weston's square face as he studied the freighter's shabby exterior. "I think I'm probably doing you a favour, Mr Hazard—that old bucket doesn't look safe to fly."

"Think what you like," Donn said abruptly, turning away. "I'm going to call my lawyer."

He strode off towards the office building with some semblance of his usual assurance, but Jan was not deceived and the anger he felt towards the bailiff increased. It was fortunate that Ozburt, a trusted friend, was on the control deck of the *Culcheth*—because not many people would have agreed to the reckless scheme he was about to put into action.

"What do you think, young man?" Weston said to Jan. "Do you reckon that ship will be able to reach the breaker's yard under its own power?"

"It's doubtful," Jan said, keeping to himself the knowledge that underneath the *Culcheth*'s grimy surface were gleaming and well-maintained power and control systems. "By the way, we were testing the electrics on the rocket ship when you arrived and the circuits are still live." He paused to let the lie sink in—there were no electrical components in the *Seeker*.

"What of it?"

"There's a risk of fire. Would you like me to go on board and switch everything off, just in case?"

Weston shrugged. "I guess so—it's not as if you were going to fly away."

"True," Jan said, smiling to conceal the fact that his heart had begun to pound. He walked to the transporter, his movements studiedly casual, and stepped up on to the trailer platform. The *Seeker* suddenly seemed huge, towering far above him. Jan climbed on the toeholds set into the crimson fuselage, reached the open canopy of the cockpit and swung himself inside. As soon as he was in the pilot's seat, lying on his back because of the rocket ship's vertical attitude, he raised his wrist communicator to his lips.

"Ozburt," he whispered, urgently, "can you hear me?" To his relief, Ozburt answered immediately.

"What's the matter, Jan?" Ozburt said. "You sound like you've got problems."

"That's the understatement of the century. The bailiffs have come and they want to impound everything Dad has."

"Aw, *no!* I'm sorry, Jan. If only they'd waited another day everything would have been . . ."

"Everything is going to be fine," Jan cut in. "I'm in the *Seeker* right now, and it will take more than a few county officials to stop me."

"But . . . but what about your Dad?"

"I'm going to leave for Verdia without him," Jan said grimly. "There's nothing else for it."

"Be reasonable," Ozburt pleaded. "It'll take an hour to get your ship on board the *Culcheth*, and by that time . . ."

"I'm not waiting an hour," Jan said. "I'm taking off right now—and so are you."

"But no matter where you land to do the loading they'll catch up on us."

"Who said anything about landing?" Jan closed the rocket ship's canopy as he spoke. "I'll meet you upstairs. Follow me up and we'll rendezvous at a thousand metres."

There was a shocked silence before Ozburt spoke again. "That's a crazy idea, Jan. It's too dangerous."

"What's the matter, Ozburt? Losing your nerve?"

"No, but I think you've lost your mind. You've never even flown that . . ."

"There's no time to argue," Jan snapped as, from the corner of his eye, he saw Weston begin to gesticulate at him. "I'm counting on you, Ozburt. My brother is counting on you, too—so don't let us down."

Without waiting for Ozburt's reply, Jan strapped himself in and initiated the firing sequence for the *Seeker*'s rocket motor. As his hands darted across the control panel he glanced down at the ground and saw the stocky figure of the bailiff running towards the transporter.

I wouldn't advise you to get too close, Jan thought as he punched the firing button.

There was a rumble from below as the tail pipes spat out flame and an instant later Weston came into view again, this time running in the opposite direction. Farther away, Donn appeared at the door to the office building.

"Sorry about this, Dad," Jan murmured, "but it has to be done."

The little ship trembled and smoke rose up on all sides as the searing exhaust from its motor set fire to the transporter vehicle. Jan waited until he was sure the plastic clamps holding the *Seeker* in place had been burned through, then he pushed the throttle fully forward.

The crimson ship ascended on a pillar of white fire which reduced the transporter to a tangle of glowing metal in a few seconds.

Grateful for the long hours he had put in on the flight simulator, Jan held the ship vertical while its speed built up. By turning his head he was able to see the gleaming expanses of the spaceport falling away beneath him. A plume of smoke from the blazing transporter was drifting across the field. The thunder of the rocket motor close behind him was overpowering. He picked out the rust-stained shape of the *Culcheth* and gave a sigh of relief as he saw it lift clear of the ground.

"Hurry up, Ozburt," he shouted towards his communicator. "I'm burning up an awful lot of fuel."

At a height of one thousand metres he throttled back until the ship was hanging motionless, gyroscopically balanced on a tongue of fire. The seconds seemed to stretch out into agonising hours as the *Culcheth*, rising easily on its gravity inverters, floated skywards and gradually overtook the *Seeker*.

Jan saw the familiar corroded hull slide upwards past him, its vastness blotting out the sun, and—guiding and controlling the *Seeker* almost by instinct—he manoeuvred closer to the open cargo door. Ozburt had extended the loading crane to catch the rocket, but the suction cup at its tip was a small and difficult target. Twice Jan thought he had steered the *Seeker*'s pointed nose into it, only to discover that he was again drifting free.

On the third attempt he saw the bright red prow enter the cone, and a tremor went through the little craft as it was clamped in place. The two ships were now locked together. Not giving himself time to think about what would happen if the suction cup were to fail, Jan closed down his rocket engine.

Its thunder died instantly, and he was left hanging in eerie silence a full kilometre above the Earth's surface.

As the crane retracted and drew him into the cargo hold, Jan took a sombre and lingering look at the sunlit hugeness of the North American continent, which was slowly being cut off from his view. He had previously convinced himself that he and his father had allowed for every eventuality, for every threat that the mission to Verdia could pose, and yet he had faced unexpected danger even before getting clear of his home world.

Was it possible that he was being foolishly over-confident in his plan to tackle the Killer Planet single-handed? Was he destined to die on Verdia as so many others had done before him?

It's too late to ask those questions, he told himself as the comparative darkness of the cargo hold closed around him. *It's too late—because there's no going back.*

Chapter 3

For a moment Jan found himself almost unable to see, his eyes having been adjusted to the dazzling sunshine outside, then he began to discern the familiar details of the cargo hold interior—the latticed stanchions, the wall-mounted fuse boxes, the myriad pipe and cable runs associated with the ship's various systems.

He opened the *Seeker*'s canopy, climbed down the rocket ship's side and jumped down on to the metal deck. The first dangerous hurdle of the voyage had been passed, but there was no time for rest or self-congratulation. He and Ozburt had made an illegal flight--an action which would not have escaped the attention of Aerospace Control—and fast interceptors would already be on their way to place the *Culcheth* under arrest. If he failed to make the warp jump to Verdia within a very few minutes the whole episode would end in an ignominious return to the Jacksonville field under escort.

Jan sprinted up the narrow metal stair which zigzagged through the top levels of the ship to the control deck situated in the prow. He was met by Ozburt, whose normal ruddy complexion had faded to an anxious pallor. Behind Ozburt the view panels shone with brilliant vistas of the Florida coast and the sunlit Atlantic ocean.

"I never want to do anything like that again—it took years off my life," Ozburt blurted, running the words together in his agitation. "We're in big trouble, Jan, and

22

that's even *before* they find out neither of us is old enough to hold a pilot's licence."

"I know that," Jan replied. "That's why we've got to warp out of here right now."

"But you can't . . ."

"Don't use that word to me," Jan cut in. "The only thing I *can't* do is let Bari and my father down."

"But there's something you don't . . ."

"Ozburt, I'm not throwing away two years of work." Jan crossed the deck, dropped into the seat at the control console and began keying the galactic coordinates of Verdia into the warp-drive computer. "As soon as we get to Verdia you can launch me in the *Seeker* and warp straight back home again. Thirty minutes should do it, and you can explain to everybody that I forced you to . . ."

Jan stopped speaking as there was an unexpected sound from the rear of the control room. He spun round and his eyebrows rose in surprise as he saw Petra Moir emerging from the galley cubicle. She was wearing a tangerine one-piece suit and was sipping from a plastibulb of coffee.

"Petra!" Jan pressed the back of a hand to his forehead. "I didn't know you were on board."

Ozburt nodded vigorously. "That's what I was trying to tell you."

"What difference does it make?" Petra said lightly. "I've been on interstellar hops before."

Jan glanced at Ozburt. "Yes, but Verdia is a prohibited destination. We're going to have to dodge patrol ships and things might get a bit . . ."

"Jan Hazard!" Petra's blue eyes beaconed her sudden anger. "A moment ago you were saying that nothing in this universe would stop you rescuing your brother. What has changed? Am I supposed to be a helpless swooning female straight out of a Victorian novel?"

"Of course not," Jan replied, his thoughts a swirl of confusion as he tried to deal with two conflicting instincts. "It's just that I don't like the idea of taking you into danger."

"That's great," Ozburt said indignantly. "You didn't worry about taking *me* into danger, did you?"

"It wasn't like that."

"Jan, if you don't stop arguing and actually *do* something you'll never even see Verdia." Petra's calm, matter-of-fact tones were more effective than a shout as she pointed at the radar display. "I'd say you have about thirty seconds to make up your mind."

Jan glanced at the screen and saw three fast-moving blips closing in on the *Culcheth*'s position. He knew they represented interceptors which, if they got to within five hundred metres, would be able to override the *Culcheth*'s computers and assume command of the ship by remote control. Lips moving silently in defiance, he finished keying in Verdia's coordinates and slammed the palm of his hand down on the red warp-activator button.

The huge ship seemed to lurch as the warp jump was made. The three young people on the *Culcheth*'s control deck experienced a moment of giddiness and dislocation, a peculiar tingling sensation as though an invisible wave had swept through them, subtly rearranging every molecule of their bodies. Petra gave an involuntary gasp as the sunny panorama of Earth disappeared from the view screens and was replaced on the instant by the feature-less white disk of an alien planet, seen from a distance of a thousand kilometres.

They were looking at the inscrutable face of Verdia—the Killer Planet—framed in the utter blackness of space.

"There it is," Jan breathed, trying to suppress the feeling of butterflies in his stomach. "Just think—my brother is down there somewhere."

"And I'm up here somewhere." Ozburt's voice sounded strained. "Would you mind letting us have some gravity?"

Jan had forgotten that the hyperspace jump would take the *Culcheth* into zero-gravity conditions. He looked over his shoulder and saw that, although Petra had secured herself by gripping a table, Ozburt had drifted clear of the deck. His outsized hands and feet were circling frantically as he tried to keep himself in a vertical attitude.

"Sorry," Jan said. He turned the artificial gravity control, restoring Ozburt's weight and at the same time quelling the fluttering sensation of lightness in his own stomach. Ozburt dropped heavily to the deck, landed off balance and sat down with a thud.

"Trust you," Petra said to him with a laugh. "You looked like a toy balloon that had..." She broke off as a man's voice crashed from the emergency communications speaker.

"This is the Stellar Quarantine Authority," it said. "You have entered a prohibited volume of space. One of the Authority's patrol ships is on its way to interrogate you and, if necessary, impound your vessel. You are instructed to hold your present position until contacted."

"It didn't take them long," Jan said, jumping up from his chair. "You take over, Ozburt. Head for the northern pole. I'll be ready for the launch when you get there."

"I'll go with you." Petra put her coffee bulb aside. "I can get the *Seeker* on to the launching cradle."

Jan nodded his gratitude and ran to the stair, with Petra close behind. Their high-speed descent was made all the more tricky when a sudden increase in their apparent weight showed that Ozburt had activated the normal-space drive and was hurling the ship towards Verdia's north pole. They clattered down the final flight of steps into the cargo hold, where the *Seeker* was still suspended from the beam crane.

Jan went to the crane's control panel and began lowering and manoeuvring the rocket ship down into a horizontal position with its nose facing the cargo door. An undercarriage like that of an aircraft would have spoiled its streamlining, therefore when the *Seeker* was taking off horizontally it had to be laid in a wheeled cradle which it left behind when it became airborne. Petra, who was familiar with the routine, guided the ship accurately into the cradle, pushing or pulling the crimson fuselage as necessary. In less than a minute the *Seeker* was securely nested in the cradle and the rocket-powered descent to the surface of the Killer Planet was about to begin.

Jan left the crane's control panel and crossed the hold to Petra. "Thanks for all your help," he said. He held out his hand, feeling strangely awkward and self-conscious, but she pushed it aside impulsively and put her arms around him.

"Go to it, Jan," she urged as they embraced. "Give it everything you've got."

"I'll do that," he said. "Now you'd better get out of here—Ozburt has to bleed all the air out of the hold before he can open the cargo door."

Petra nodded, kissed him briefly but warmly and ran towards the stair. Jan stared after her for a second, realising that the friendly affection he had always felt for Petra was being displaced by a more powerful emotion, then he climbed up the side of the rocket ship. He was in the process of stepping into the cockpit when Ozburt's voice, harsh with urgency, crackled from the intercom speaker.

"Get a move on, Jan! The interceptor has caught up on us and it's coming in fast. Our controls are going to be enslaved at any second unless I take evasive action."

An instant later the floor of the cargo bay tilted wildly and a chorus of creaks came from the surrounding structure as the *Culcheth* was thrown into a high-G manoeuvre for which it had not been designed. Jan, with one foot in the *Seeker's* cockpit, was taken unawares and could not react fast enough to avoid plunging downwards. His jaw struck the rim of the rocket ship's windscreen with all the force of an uppercut delivered by a professional boxer.

He collapsed into the cramped space of the cockpit, consciousness fleeing amid a dazzling burst of fireworks which rapidly faded into blackness.

The next few minutes were like a fragmentary dream for Jan, a kaleidoscope of disjointed images and sounds . . .

He was vaguely aware of Ozburt's voice, remote and meaningless, reaching across what seemed to be a million light years . . . *interceptor still on my tail, Jan, and closing in fast* . . . pain, pulsing pain and a screaming sense of urgency . . . there was something he had to do, something vital, but what was it? . . . *are you ready, Jan?* . . . ready for what? . . . *if I don't open the cargo door right now it's going to be too late* . . .

A glimpse of Petra's blue eyes regarding him anxiously . . . strong hands, half-lifting half-guiding him into a seat . . . *anything wrong down there, Jan? Answer me, answer me* . . .

The sound of the canopy being slammed shut . . . Petra's

27

voice, firm and clear, giving orders . . . a wash of brilliance as the massive cargo door slid open, admitting the light of an alien sun . . . shuddering vibrations and a fierce burst of gut-wrenching acceleration . . .

Jan clung to consciousness, forcing his eyes to remain open, but ages seemed to pass before he understood what was happening . . .

He was in the cockpit of the *Seeker*, dropping down towards the unknown perils of the Killer Planet.

And beside him, gamely struggling to master the rocket ship's controls, was Petra Moir.

Chapter 4

"Petra!" Jan shook his head groggily and forced himself into an upright position. "You . . . you aren't supposed to be here."

"Somebody had to get the *Seeker* out of the cargo hold before the controls were taken away from Ozburt," Petra said, her gaze fixed on the tilting and rapidly expanding view of Verdia directly ahead. "And you were too busy having a snooze. Are you all right now?"

"I guess so." There was a crushing pain in Jan's head, and he felt cold and nauseated, but he was again in control of his thoughts and actions.

"That's good—because I'm finding this thing harder to fly than I expected." Petra spoke calmly, but a slight tremor in her voice alerted Jan to the fact that she was in difficulties as the rocket ship plunged into the upper levels of Verdia's atmosphere.

"I'll take over now," he said. He held the control wheel steady while Petra clambered into the small storage space at the rear of the cockpit, then he slid over into the pilot's seat. While he was strapping himself in, Petra twisted her way into the passenger seat and did likewise. Until that point the drop towards Verdia had been smooth and silent, but now the ship was beginning to stir and come to life as it reached the denser air strata. A faint but gradually increasing whistling sound testified to its speed through the atmosphere.

The descent through Verdia's cloud cover was a pro-
longed series of fierce jolts which tested the *Seeker*'s
structure to the limit. Jan's arms were aching from the
strain of keeping the little ship under control, and there
were times when he feared that the supertough plastic
of the wings might snap from overload as they hit the
bottom of an airpocket.

"We have to touch down close to the planet's north
pole," he said during a lull in the atmospheric buffeting.
"That would be tough enough in an ordinary spacecraft,
but it's worse in the *Seeker* because we have no navigational
instruments to help us find our way down."

"Why's that?"

"They'd have to be made of metal, and . . ." Jan swore as
an unusually powerful gust turned the little ship on its side
and he had to fight to bring it level. "We know that metal
disturbs the planet's magnetic field . . . attracts all the
lightning . . . so the *Seeker* is built almost entirely of plastics.
It will be able to land safely—we hope!"

Petra glanced all around the cockpit, noting the complete
absence of metal fittings. "But what about the rocket
motor?"

"Ceramic. Modern ceramics are as tough and as heat-
proof as many metals. The motor is the least of our
worries—I'm only praying the ship doesn't start to break
up around us."

Petra fell silent, deciding not to risk distracting Jan from
the task of controlling the *Seeker* in its downward plunge
through Verdia's cloudy atmosphere. The ship was dropping through the greyness at hundreds of kilometres an
hour, only gradually losing speed because of friction with
the air, and at this rate there was little time for conversation.

A few hectic minutes was all it would take for the *Seeker* to reach ground level. In comparison, Ozburt—in the mother ship's drifting orbital calmness—could have been at a Sunday picnic. There was no doubt that he would soon be arrested by the Stellar Quarantine Authority, but after questioning he would probably be sent home to spend the coming night securely tucked up in bed.

Jan's face was pale with tension and fatigue as he fought the *Seeker*'s controls. He was in good physical condition, but he had been weakened by the stunning blow to his chin, and the turbulence of Verdia's atmosphere was draining his strength. It was as if the Killer Planet was a giant living entity which had sensed their approach and was doing its best to destroy the two human intruders before they even set foot on the surface. Jan muttered grimly to himself as the ship gave a particularly violent lurch, then all at once they were through the cloud ceiling and a jungle-covered landscape was spread out below.

Ahead of the plunging craft there appeared faint geometric markings which confirmed that it was close to the ancient ruin of a city which had been discovered by the development team. The patterns were swelling rapidly in the forward windscreen, making it apparent that something would have to be done quickly to avoid a crash.

"Pull her up!" Petra shouted. "Do you need any help?"

"I can manage," Jan replied.

The cloud ceiling had been so low that the craft was now skimming the tops of the higher trees. Jan hauled back on the control column, bringing the *Seeker*'s nose sharply upwards, and in the same instant fired the rocket motor. The sudden surge of power converted what would have been a fatal stall for an ordinary aircraft into a landing manoeuvre which Jan had practised many times on the computer simulator.

The *Seeker* swept into a vertical attitude, gyroscopically balanced on its fiery exhaust, and sank tail-first down into the sea of thick foliage. Leaves, fronds and sections of smoking vine fountained away on all sides as the force of the exhaust tore into the vegetation, then the ship touched solid ground. Jan cut the engine. Petra and he lay perfectly still for a moment, relieved at having reached the ground in safety.

"We made it," Jan breathed. "I wouldn't like to go through that again—not *ever*."

"We'd better start thinking about what comes next." Petra began unbuckling her safety harness.

Jan did likewise. "The main thing is that Dad was right about the *Seeker*'s non-metallic construction—the ship isn't attracting any lightning."

"It might be attracting other things, though. We're in a jungle, Jan, and it isn't even an Earth jungle—there could be *anything* waiting for us out there. We'd better get ourselves ready to face it."

"You're right," Jan replied, pulling open the canopy.

Warm and intensely humid air swirled through the cockpit, bringing with it a medley of sounds from the jungle —raucous cries from unseen birds, the chittering of small animals, and occasional deep-toned bellows from unknown larger species.

"So far so good," Jan said, turning to look at Petra. "But now there's the problem of what to do with you."

"What problem?" There was more than a hint of exasperation in Petra's voice. "I don't see any problem."

"Petra, you can *hear* what it's like out there in the jungle. This is a dangerous place and I can't expect you to . . ."

"Listen to me, Jan Hazard—I want to get this thing settled once and for all," Petra interrupted. "There are only two courses open to us at this stage. The first one is that you can take off again immediately, surrender to the quarantine police and forget all about rescuing Bari. You don't want to do that, do you?"

"No."

"Good! At least we've got that much settled. The second option is that we stop wasting valuable time and go and find your brother." Petra finished unfastening her harness. "And as for the danger from wild animals—don't forget I'm a better shot than you with the bow. Now, are we agreed that you will stop fussing over me like a mother hen and concentrate on the job we have to do?"

Jan hesitated briefly, then gave her a smile of gratitude. "It's a deal," he said. "And thanks for putting me straight."

"We'll make a good team," Petra replied, returning his smile. "Now, if you'll hand me the spare survival pack we can get started."

Jan took the two lightweight containers from the rear of the cockpit and gave one to Petra. She swung herself out of the cockpit with a single lithe movement and worked her way down the side of the crimson ship. With his own pack slung over his shoulder, Jan went out after her, closing the canopy to keep out the rain and unwelcome wildlife, then climbed down to the ground.

The blackened area of the landing site was still smoking, but there was no risk of fire spreading—every leaf and branch of the surrounding jungle dripped with moisture which was condensing out of Verdia's saturated air. Thunder rumbled intermittently in the distance and every now and then the scene was illuminated by varicoloured flashes of lightning.

"This is a real hell-hole, isn't it?" Jan said solemnly, looking all about him. "It would be damn hard for anybody to survive for long here without a lot of supplies."

Petra, who had been busy opening her pack, gave him a level stare. "I never met your brother, but from what you told me about him he's a natural survivor. Right?"

"Right."

"And we're here on the assumption that he *has* survived. Isn't that so?"

Jan nodded, forcing a smile. "Bari has to be alive around here, somewhere, and we're going to find him."

He opened his own pack and took from it a green one-piece coverall which was light, tough and waterproof. After he had pulled it on over his shirt and slacks—reminders that less than an hour ago he had been enjoying the Florida summer—and had zipped it up to his neck he felt better prepared to face the jungle.

Petra, now similarly attired, drew the next item out of her pack—a belt on which were slung a knife and a two-edged sword. She strapped them on and partially withdrew the grey-bladed sword from its sheath.

"More plastic," she said, laughing. "I feel as if I'd been kitted out by some fast-food restaurant. Where's my plastic spoon?"

"Those weapons are as good as best-quality steel," Jan assured her. "The main difference is they're a bit lighter."

When he had fastened his own belt he added to it a pouch containing compressed rations and some medical supplies. Finally, he stooped and brought out a plastic bow and a quiver of tubular arrows, a weapon with which he had practised assiduously for many hours under Petra's tuition.

The laminated bow was of standard hunting pattern, but the arrows were of his father's own design and far from conventional. Each was in fact a slim solid-fuel rocket, the propellant of which was ignited by the sudden acceleration of the arrow's release. The plastic fletchings were coloured yellow, orange or red according to the quantity and power of the fuel the arrows contained. Jan had no idea of what dangerous beasts the Verdian jungle might harbour, but he believed that he and Petra were well equipped to deal with them.

Petra finished kitting out at the same time as Jan. She pinned up her hair in a businesslike fashion and covered it with the jungle hat which had come with the supply pack. As he watched her calm preparations for facing the unknown the thought came to Jan that he had been lucky that fate had given him Petra as a companion—and perhaps that was a good omen for the rest of the mission.

"Are we ready to set off?" he said.

"*I've* been ready for ages." Petra examined him with a humorously critical eye. "And I must say I look better in this kind of gear than you do—perhaps I should assume command of this whole expedition."

"Field promotions have to be earned, and so far we haven't seen any action." Slinging his quiver and bow over his shoulder, Jan took a small compass from his pocket. Its needle was the tiny fragment of metal he had risked bringing on the desperate venture. At this proximity to Verdia's north pole the needle was standing almost vertically on its pivot, but he managed to get a rough bearing which would help them find their way back to the ship.

"Well, the first thing we have to do is make our way into

that ruined city we saw from the air," Jan said. "That was where the first landing was made by the engineering group, and the records show that the SEF detachment touched down in roughly the same area."

"Do you think the ones who survived would have stayed in the same place where all those terrible things happened?"

"Probably not, but I'm betting that if survivors from either group had decided to move to a safer or pleasanter area they would have left direction signs behind them. Don't forget they wouldn't have realised that the Council was going to sell them down the river—they would have been expecting a full-scale rescue mission to come after them."

Petra nodded. "That makes sense."

With one last glance at the *Seeker*—its slick crimson curvatures so incongruous in the prehistoric environment of the jungle—Jan and Petra unsheathed their swords and moved off into the gloom. As natives of Florida, they were no strangers to swampy wilderness—such as the Everglades —but nothing could have prepared them for the actuality of the Verdian jungle. Trees, vines, giant flowers, thorny shrubs, mosses and waist-high grasses fought for every inch of space. So virulent was their growth that in some places the movement was discernible—the tendrils of climbing plants could be seen blindly probing for their grip on trees; carnivorous flowers closed with audible snaps as they engulfed their prey.

"We should blaze a trail to help us find our way back," Jan said. He used his sword to slice an area of bark off a tree, revealing a patch of white, but within seconds the bark was visibly spreading inwards to repair the wound.

"The books didn't mention anything like that," he

grumbled. "I guess we'll have to rely on our sense of direction."

"It's a pity you didn't bring the silly books with you," Petra said. "You could have torn them up and left a trail."

Their progress was aided by the fact that Verdia's gravity was slightly less than that of Earth, but the heat and humidity were such that within minutes their clothes were soaked with sweat. The air was filled with the buzzing of insects, and at almost every step small rodents and scorpion-like creatures darted out of their path. Praying that none of the latter were poisonous, they went onwards at a steady pace, the deceptively dull grey swords at the ready.

They had travelled only a short distance when an un-pleasant and unnerving idea occurred to them—they began to suspect they were not alone.

Petra was the first to acknowledge her growing sense of alarm. Her suspicions had developed gradually as she began to notice stealthy, shadowy flickers of movement at the edges of her vision. For a while she was almost able to convince herself that her nerves were playing tricks. Every time she glanced around, sword poised to strike, there was only the wall of vegetation and watchful pockets of dark-ness. She was torn between the desire to utter a warning to Jan and the possibility of causing a needless alarm, but the dilemma was resolved when Jan came closer and nudged her arm.

"Do you think we've got company?" he whispered.

"I didn't want to mention it until I was sure," she replied, "but I think we have."

"I wonder what it is."

"There's no way to tell—but we'd better be ready to give it hell if it comes too close."

They pressed ahead through the dripping greenery, during which time the silent follower gradually became bolder. It came closer and its movements became more leisurely, and finally Jan and Petra got a good view of a manlike figure covered in long black hair. Much lighter in build than a gorilla, the creature moved with disturbing speed and agility. It disappeared silently into the gloom ahead of them.

"Yikes!" Petra exclaimed. "What a nasty-looking brute!"

"I know," Jan said uneasily. "I only hope it's hanging around out of curiosity—and not hunger." He picked up a mossy stick and threw it towards where the skulking figure had last been seen. There was no response other than the patter of water droplets falling from disturbed leaves. The lack of reaction strengthened his hope that the creature posed no threat to them, but he remained on the alert and kept his sword at the ready, just in case. And without being too obvious about it he tried to make sure their rate of progress did not slacken off. It may have been his concern about keeping up speed which brought it to his notice that Petra was limping slightly.

"Have you hurt your ankle?" he said, trying not to sound worried.

Petra signalled for him to keep moving. "A thorn came through my boot. It isn't too bad, though—I'll pull it out as soon as we reach a good clear space."

"It would be better if we do keep going, but maybe your foot should be looked at before it gets worse."

Petra shook her head. "Not while we're hedged in like this. Not with that rotten Abominable Snowman about."

"Okay—it's up to you," Jan said, resuming the task of clearing vines and creepers out of their way with his sword.

About fifteen minutes later they came to an area where the jungle abruptly thinned out and they saw ahead the ruins of buildings. The tumbled columns and broken walls were extensively covered with vines, but it was evident that they were made of polished marble and had been sculpted to a high standard of craftsmanship.

"Hey! This must have been quite a place in its day," Petra exclaimed. "It must have been a bit like ancient Athens or Rome. Gosh, who'd have expected to find anything like this on a jungle planet?"

"The Verdians must have been really civilised . . . really *advanced* . . ." Jan surveyed the enigmatic, mist-shrouded remains of once-proud buildings. "I wonder what happened to them. The place looks like it was flattened by a nuclear bomb."

"Or an earthquake."

"Whatever it was, I'm glad I wasn't here at the time," Jan said, his voice hushed with awe. "I wonder if we'll find any clues about what happened."

"I'm not even going to think about that until I get this damned thorn out of my foot." Petra sat down on a block of masonry and began to ease off her left boot.

Jan scanned the area in all directions, satisfying himself that there was enough open ground to ensure they could not be surprised by any wandering wild beasts. And then, fascinated by the mystery of the place, he walked towards the nearest of the ruined buildings. He had to pick his way around several large clumps of purple-flowered shrubs which were growing up through a layer of yellow moss. He then found that his path was barred by some sizeable boulders, but they were not high enough to form any real obstacle. His gazed fixed on the intriguing ruins, he placed his left hand on a boulder and vaulted over it—but the leap was never completed.

His hand sank into a yielding wetness which felt exactly like a cold mouth.

Horrified, Jan fell sideways and saw that what he had taken to be a boulder was actually a huge slug-like creature. *No, no, NO!* he thought in panic as he saw that his hand had sunk deeply into the glutinous tissues of the monster. He had been deceived by one of Nature's oldest tricks—the mimicry by which slow-moving carnivores capture their prey. He tried to pull his hand away and made the terrifying discovery that the slug-monster was too strong for him. It was exerting powerful suction on his hand and wrist—ripples coursing over its surface as it did so—and his arm was inexorably being drawn farther into its interior.

His face distorted by fear and revulsion, Jan tightened his grip on his sword and struck at the monster's grey body. The keen blade went deep into the rubbery tissues, but the wound closed up immediately, clamping the sword in a pliant but relentless hold.

Jan struggled with all his strength to pull it free, but to no avail. His left arm was now engulfed up to the elbow and was being drawn farther in with each passing second. As he fought to withdraw the sword he raised his eyes and saw that the situation was even worse than he had realised.

The black-gorilla creature—no longer timid or elusive —had appeared on the scene and was advancing on him, obviously emboldened by the fact that he was a helpless prisoner. Now that he could see the alien properly, he was aware that its mouth was a vertical gash lined with razored yellow teeth. Saliva dripped from its jaws as it drew closer.

Jan released his grip on the sword and reached for his

knife, then came the realisation that it would be even less effective. He writhed and twisted as he tried to pull his left arm out of the slug-monster's greedy maw, but all that happened was that his arm was sucked in deeper. A burning sensation in his hand told him that the monster's acidic digestive fluids were beginning to eat into his skin.

The gorilla-creature, now capering and snuffling in its eagerness, leapt forward and dug its clawed fingers into Jan's shoulder. It raised its head in preparation for a lunging bite, and the sickening stench of its breath wafted around him—then Jan heard a peculiar sound. It was a combination of an explosive hiss and a *thud* like an axe being driven deep into a tree stump.

The gorilla-creature screamed and fell away from Jan. He saw that a smoking arrow with yellow fletchings had transfixed one of its thighs. It dropped to the ground, still screaming and sobbing, and crawled away. Jan looked to the right and saw Petra, bow in hand, running towards him.

She arrived at his side, eyes widening in horror as she saw that he was in the process of being devoured by the slug-monster. She whipped out her sword, and was about to attack the living grey mass with it when Jan raised a warning hand.

"A blade won't work," he shouted. "Try an arrow! A red one! Fire it in!"

In a single swift movement she drew an arrow from her quiver, notched it into the bow and fired it into the slug-creature's rippling grey bulk. The arrow flared brilliantly and sank out of sight, burrowing far down into the quivering tissues. Foul-smelling greasy smoke erupted from behind it.

There was a seemingly endless moment when it appeared

that the miniature rocket had been effortlessly absorbed, then the slug-monster gave a convulsive heave.

Suddenly Jan was free.

He leaped to his feet, his face pale with shock, wiping a coating of acidic slime from his left hand. The skin was red and already beginning to blister.

"Are you all right?" Petra said urgently.

Jan managed something close to a smile. "I will be— thanks to you."

"What about that *thing?*" Petra nodded towards the stricken gorilla-creature which was dragging itself away from the scene. "I had to aim low—its legs were the only clear shot I could get."

Jan eyed the beast with hatred and revulsion. "I'll finish the brute off," he said, picking up his fallen bow. Taking a yellow-feathered arrow from his quiver, he nocked it onto the bowstring, drew the bow and took aim at the black hairy form, which was grunting and whimpering as it tried to make its escape. He maintained the firing stance for perhaps ten seconds, then slowly lowered the weapon.

"I can't kill it," he said. "*We're* the intruders on its world. We came here to rescue my brother—not to go hunting for big game."

Petra nodded. "It's no longer a threat—so let's keep moving."

Jan glanced down and saw that she was again wearing both of her boots. "It didn't take you long to get the thorn out."

"I've got the hands of a surgeon."

"Lucky for me . . ." Jan eyed Petra solemnly for a moment, then put his arms around her. "You saved my life."

"You can do the same for me sometime," Petra said,

briefly returning the embrace. "Now, let's get going."

"Good idea!" Jan replaced the unused arrow in his quiver. He turned and pulled his sword out of the grey bulk of the slug-monster's body, which was settling and wrinkling like a slowly deflating balloon.

"We've learned a valuable lesson here," he said, staring down at the dying creature with distaste. "From now on we don't assume that *anything* on this God-forsaken world is harmless."

"*Two* valuable lessons," Petra corrected. "From now on we must keep in sight of each other at all times."

"Agreed." Jan dried the blade of his sword on a tuft of grass and pulled his jungle hat down tightly on his head. "Now, let's see what this city can tell us."

Chapter 5

In spite of the profusion of creeping plants and mosses, the going was much easier now that there was level pavement under their feet. They picked their way along the ruins of broad avenues, at times speculating about what kind of calamity had wiped out such an advanced and thriving culture. Rows of broken columns projecting from the ground-hugging vegetation increasingly reminded Jan of classical ruins on Earth, augmenting his sympathy for the long-dead Verdians.

The humid, murky atmosphere and the frequent stabs of lightning between the ground and the low cloud ceiling added to the pair's sense of foreboding. It was impossible as yet to know what the Verdians themselves had looked like, but from the proportions of occasional doors and windows which had remained intact it seemed possible that the dead race had been about the same size and shape as human beings.

"I wish we could find a few statues," Petra said. "It would be like meeting the Verdians face to face."

Jan nodded. "That's a thought. I wish we had a camera with us—just in case."

"I've got a pencil, and I can make sketches."

A few minutes later they had to skirt around a rectangular opening where a section of pavement had collapsed into what must have been a tunnel. An unusually bright flurry of lightning bolts lit up the scene for a moment, enabling them to see the remains of enigmatic machines in the subterranean dimness. The ruined equipment was heavily stained with rust.

"It looks a bit like a power station," Petra said. "You can imagine workers scuttling around down there and . . ."

"Wait a minute!" Jan cut in, his words fading away rapidly into the surrounding gloom. "That looks like ordinary rust on those machines! In fact, I'm *sure* that's what it is!"

"What of it?"

"Remember the official theory about what caused all the disasters on this world?"

Petra looked thoughtful. "Yes, something about our vehicles and machinery attracting lightning."

"It was electromagnetic forces, actually, but lightning is near enough."

"If lightning is near enough," Petra said impatiently, "why don't they just *say* lightning instead of dragging in long words?"

"Because electromagnetism covers other forces which can't be seen, but which are just as powerful and . . ." Jan took a deep breath. "We're getting away from the point, Petra. According to the theory, metal machinery could *never* have existed on Verdia—but those machines down in the tunnel are covered in ordinary rust. They must be made of metal! And if the Verdians routinely used metal artifacts . . ."

"Whatever destroyed *our* forces must have come on the scene more recently!" Petra glanced up at the sullen clouds. "Could the climate of the planet have changed in the last hundred years or so?"

"I don't know," Jan replied. "This place is a bigger mystery to me than ever."

Suppressing an unaccountable feeling that the threat against them had somehow become more immediate, they moved on. Frowning, their eyes constantly scanning their surroundings, they carefully made their way through mounds of rubble and strangely-coloured vegetation. An indeterminate time later they picked out the spire-like out-line of a large spaceship jutting above some trees in the middle distance.

"That's a civilian craft!" Jan gave a whoop of excitement. "We're getting somewhere at last! That ship must be sitting where the engineering team landed—maybe we'll find a sign telling us where they've gone."

They worked their way towards the ship, occasionally hacking through curtains of vines, and scrambling over piles of masonry which had been upturned by massive roots. Eventually they reached the edge of an area where the vegetation was comparatively sparse—an indication that some clearing work had once been done—enabling them to see perhaps four hundred metres ahead.

The scene was one of utter desolation.

The giant spaceship was a rusting hulk which appeared to have been struck by a thousand lightning bolts. Its surface was covered with gashes and scars, where molten metal had run like candle wax, and the heavy plating had been blasted off in places to expose the ribs of the underly-ing structure. Jan tried to visualise what could have wreaked such damage, but his imagination baulked at the task.

Petra looked awe-struck as her eyes took in the extent of the destruction. "I hadn't realised it would be as bad as that," she whispered. "Something really *awful* must have happened here."

Jan nodded, his face grim. "I think we'd better prepare ourselves for some ugly sights when we get closer."

As they went farther into the cleared space around the ship they saw that the area was littered with derelict earth-moving equipment—bulldozers, diggers, trucks, dumpers. All of the machines were streaked with the corrosion which spread so rapidly in Verdia's warm, moisture-laden atmosphere, and many were overgrown with moss and grass.

"They look like they've been here for ages," Petra said, unconsciously lowering her voice. "Can it only have been two years?"

"Two years is a hell of a long time in a place like this," Jan replied, wondering what state of health his brother and other survivors would be in after existing for so long in such unfavourable conditions.

He and Petra continued to advance cautiously, side by side, and had covered only a short distance when they discovered the first of the skeletons.

The remains of the development engineers had been picked clean, reduced to pallid bones by the jungle's voracious scavenger animals and insects. They lay everywhere—the skulls grinning, the shadowy eye sockets seeming to reproach the pair for having arrived too late to render assistance in their hour of need.

Controlling her natural revulsion, Petra studied the skeletal figures like a forensic scientist, looking for any kind of a clue about what had happened to them on the fatal day of the landing.

"Look," she said, touching Jan's arm, "some of the skeletons are broken up . . . crushed right into the ground . . .

47

It's as if somebody had deliberately driven right over them with the bulldozers. It's *ghastly!*"

"You're right—nothing else could have done that to them." Numbed with horror though he was by the grisly finds, Jan's mind seized on the sinister new element of the mystery of Verdia. Was it possible that some kind of terrible madness, perhaps induced by alien microbes, had afflicted the machines' operators, prompting them to hunt down and crush their fellow workers? What other reason could there have been for workers turning their machines against their colleagues in such an orgy of death and destruction?

Jan and Petra stood in silence for a moment and, in spite of the oppressive heat, they both shuddered as they took in the vistas of dread.

Only two years earlier this spot had been bustling with life and activity—now it was a nightmarish graveyard, where the only movement was the furtive skulking of rat-like alien creatures and spiders nesting in skulls. Some terrible and unknown evil force had been at work here, and now it seemed that the two young people from Earth had been incredibly brash and presumptuous in pitting themselves against it . . .

Clank! Clank-clank!

The mechanical sound came from close behind, causing them to spin round to face it.

"What the hell's that?" Jan exclaimed, features rigid with shock as he scanned the dimly lit surroundings.

"Over there!" Petra cried, pointing at one of the grass-shrouded metal hulks. *"One of the bulldozers is moving!"*

"But that's imposs . . ." Jan's voice faded as he saw that one of the mechanical monsters had indeed begun to stir.

It was rolling directly towards them, and as it burst out of

48

its covering of grass and creepers they saw that there was a skeleton leaning over the controls.

For one pounding instant they were paralysed with fear, then they instinctively linked hands and backed away, shaking their heads in appalled disbelief.

This was impossible!

There was no sound of engines—and yet the bulldozer was on the move; the skeletal figure in the control cabin could see nothing with its eyeless sockets—and yet the bulldozer was coming straight at the two young people. And it was obviously filled with deadly purpose!

Still holding hands, they ran to one side—and the bulldozer promptly changed course and came after them. They veered in the opposite direction, and again the clanking machine turned and came in pursuit.

The weapons in their limited arsenal were obviously useless against the armoured juggernaut, so the only thing to do was to flee to the comparative safety of the jungle.

Jan pointed at the nearest line of trees and Petra nodded. Separating a little in order to achieve maximum speed, they ran for the trees, leaping wildly over mounds of earth, bursting through thickets of brush and grass. Petra easily kept pace with Jan, her booted feet scarcely seeming to touch the ground.

They had covered about fifty metres when they made a fresh horrifying discovery—the lumbering machine was travelling faster than they could!

In normal circumstances they would have been able to outrun that kind of track-laying vehicle, but the bulldozer seemed to have been possessed by a demonic force which was driving it forward with supernatural speed. With an horrendous shrieking of rusted components, gloating skeleton at the controls, the bulldozer was gaining on them with every second. It was becoming quite obvious that they had no hope of winning a straight-line dash to the jungle.

"We're not going to make it this way," Jan gasped.

Petra's strained expression showed that she had already reached the same conclusion. "Start zigzagging again! The dozer is so heavy and clumsy that it's bound to lose speed when it corners."

They immediately swerved to the left and heard the juggernaut's tracks screech as it slewed around in pursuit. They changed direction several times in quick succession, each time with the bulldozer nearly on their heels, before they could accept that the new technique was not proving successful.

The machine's preternatural speed and powers were enabling it to keep pace with them—and they were rapidly becoming exhausted. At this rate they probably had only a few tens of seconds left to them before the massive steel blade at the front of the bulldozer brought them down and pulped them into the ground.

Knuckling the sweat from their eyes, they cast about desperately for a means of escape. Ahead and slightly to the left was a shallow, dish-like depression in the pavement. It was reminiscent of the place where they had seen the ancient machinery in the collapsed tunnel section, and the thought came to Petra that underground rooms and workings might be commonplace in the ancient city.

"That might be . . . a weak spot," she called out, pointing at the area of sagging pavement, her words blurred by the thick saltiness of exhaustion which was gathering in her mouth. "There might be . . . another tunnel."

"It's worth a try," Jan panted.

As if responding to a silent command, they suddenly bore to the left and sprinted across the sagging masonry. They felt the paving slabs vibrate beneath their feet, and for a moment it seemed that the whole area might collapse into the depths and take both of them with it.

With one desperate effort they threw themselves at the far rim of the depression—just as the ancient stonework gave way beneath them.

The howling, screeching bulldozer—which had been within a few paces of them—tilted and plunged down into the freshly opened cavity with a deafening crash, sending clouds of dust and pulverised rock billowing into the air. They heard and felt it butting at subterranean walls, like some kind of blind animal struggling to escape from a cage.

"That was a near one," Jan said as they got to their feet at the rim of the cavernous hole which had appeared in the ground. "I thought we were finished."

"I only hope the monster stays down there." Petra had to shout to make herself heard above the appalling noise. Tremors raced through the ground every time the bulldozer impacted with the sides of its rocky prison. Apparently driven by some malign and supernatural force, the machine showed no sign of slackening its efforts to escape. The shriek of metal grinding on rusty metal continued to assault the senses, and every now and then there was the rumble of falling earth and masonry.

Jan looked down into the clamorous turmoil. "It's bringing down a lot of broken rock. If it keeps on doing that it might be able to build a sort of ramp . . . climb out . . ."

Petra inclined her head towards the jungle's edge. "The sooner we get in among those trees the better."

They set out on legs which were still weary from running

and the unnerving din of the bulldozer gradually faded behind them as they neared the inviting cover of the dense foliage. By the time they had penetrated a kilometre into the gigantic, dripping trees they were surrounded by comparative quietness—the sound of the jungle's wild creatures no longer seemed as threatening as before—and they began to relax a little.

"I wonder if we should stop for a little while," Jan said, wiping sweat from his brow.

"There's no need—my legs feel all right again."

"It's all very well for you." Jan gave Petra a rueful glance. "Back home you spent half your time sprinting around race tracks, while I was crammed inside the *Seeker* getting weak and flabby."

"Excuses!" Petra taunted.

"Seriously though, we ought to eat something to keep up our strength," Jan said. "I can't remember the last time I even saw food."

"You're beginning to sound like Ozburt." Petra pointed at a fallen tree whose trunk offered a good place on which to sit. "Why don't you park your worn-out old body over there?"

"That looks fine—but I'm not taking any more chances." Jan drew his sword and drove the point of it into the tree in several places. The blade met with a satisfying woody resistance, so he invited Petra to be seated with an exaggerated courtly gesture.

Joining in the game, she gathered up an imaginary crinoline skirt and sat down on the natural bench. "Talking about Ozburt—where do you think he is now?"

"My guess is that he's been taken back to Jacksonville by this time."

"I wonder if he'll contact my parents and let them know what's been happening."

"He will," Jan said confidently. "You know, I see now that I've been giving Ozburt a rough deal. I'm always ribbing him or getting at him for this and that, but when the chips were down he turned out to be an absolute ace. Not many people would have had the guts—or even the ability—to back me up the way he did. Considering the way I've been treating him, I'm amazed that he stuck with Dad and me on the *Seeker* project as long as he did."

Petra gave him a sympathetic look. "We all know things haven't been easy for you."

"Thanks, but I still wish I had put things right with Ozburt before . . ." Deciding it would be better to abandon the subject, Jan opened his pouch and took out a squeeze-bulb of colourless liquid and a block of what might have been chocolate but when unwrapped proved to be a substance resembling grey plastic. He bit a corner off the block with some difficulty and began chewing.

Petra did likewise and a look of dismay appeared on her face. "My God, Jan, what's this stuff meant to *be*? It looks like old tennis shoes, it smells like old tennis shoes . . ." She scrutinised the block in her hand. "I think it actually *is* old tennis shoes."

"Eat up—it's good for you," Jan said, vainly trying to look enthusiastic. "It's loaded with good stuff . . . protein . . . and vitamins . . . and . . ."

"Old tennis shoes." Petra took a sip from her squeezebulb and her expression of distaste became even more evident. "Ugh! Sugary water!"

"For your information, that's a high-energy glucose drink—scientifically designed to keep you going."

"To the bathroom?" Petra showed her opinion of the drink by squirting some of it over Jan's boots. "Next time we go on a picnic, Jan Hazard, *I'm* packing the hamper, and I'll start off with something that's worth eating."

"Do me a favour and throw in some decent food for me," Jan said, pretending to puke. "This stuff is pretty awful, isn't it? My Dad chose the rations, and nobody can say he was planning to spoil himself on this trip."

"Still, if we'd been loaded down with goodies we might not have gotten away from the bulldozer." Petra's eyes grew sombre as she recalled the narrowness of their escape. "The skeleton at the wheel looked horrible and spooky, but we know it had nothing to do with the bulldozer coming to life. It was just the remains of the poor driver who was . . . How can things like this happen, Jan? How *could* a bulldozer come to life?"

"I've been thinking about that, and not getting very far," Jan said, toying with the unappetising foodstuff. "The official theory about Verdia . . . about planetary electro-magnetic forces somehow entering machines and making them go haywire . . . has always seemed a bit too pat to me, too easy, too much of a cop-out—but at least it was based on the laws of Nature."

"So you're saying the bulldozer was taken over by something . . . *super*natural?"

Jan shook his head. "I don't *want* to say that—it goes against everything I was ever taught—but we both know what happened back there. The dozer came after us, *hunted* us, as if it was being controlled by some kind of an evil spirit. I can't come up with a logical explanation for that, and I doubt if any of the eggheads back on Earth could, either."

"We're a long way from Earth," Petra said pensively. "It

might be that things work differently here. Perhaps the natural laws that we know, don't apply in this part of the galaxy."

"If that's true, the odds against us are worse than we imagined. I was a real smart-ass, Petra. I was so sure I had everything worked out in advance, and now . . ."

"You've done well," Petra said softly. "Your father would be proud of you."

"Thanks." Jan gave her a wry smile. "I wish I had been able to speak to him before I took off."

"He knows where you are and what you're doing."

"He'll be worried, that's for sure. You see, my mother was killed in a tourist plane crash on Cerulea when I was three. Then Bari disappeared. And now I've vanished into the same jungle without even a radio to maintain any kind of contact. Dad must feel that space is an enemy that robs him of his family, one by one. That's why he was so determined to go it alone in the *Seeker*."

"There's no need for you to feel guilty," Petra said.

Jan shrugged. "I know—but somehow I can't help it."

"Look at it this way." Petra tentatively placed her hand over Jan's. "You and I are good runners in pretty well peak physical condition, but we beat that bulldozer by only a couple of metres. Your father was detained, but if he *had* been there instead of us the monster would have caught up on him—and that fact alone justifies everything you've done."

Jan was comforted by her words and warmed by her touch. He drained his squeezebulb and threw it away into the surrounding undergrowth, causing a pitter-patter as droplets cascaded from the disturbed leaves. The grey cloud ceiling seemed lower than ever, hiding the tops of the highest trees, and sheet lightning flickered incessantly through the gloom.

"We'd better get going again," he said, rising to his feet, feeling a renewal of confidence in spite of the depressing environment. "We've barely got started on the job."

"Yes, but we're going to finish it," Petra replied as she stood up. "No matter what dirty tricks this damned planet has up its sleeve!"

Chapter 6

Almost by instinct, they had curved their path through the jungle in a northerly direction and now, through gaps in the foliage, they could see the outline of another spaceship projecting into the sky. Its smooth lines were interrupted by the bulges of weapons turrets, and it was obvious to Jan and Petra that they were approaching the area where the Stellar Expeditionary Force had tried to establish its beachhead.

"This is it," Jan said, his voice betraying his excitement. "This is where we find out where Bari has gone to."

"Great! Then we can all get out of this place." Petra spoke brightly to conceal her growing concern over Bari Hazard's probable fate. In spite of all they had learned about Verdia's inexplicable terrors, Jan was clinging to his belief that highly trained soldiers would have been able to survive where civilian workers had perished. But Petra, judging by what she had seen, found it hard to imagine *anybody* escaping alive from the kind of widespread destruction which had been visited on the engineering team. She had not expressed her fears to Jan, out of consideration for his feelings, but now there was no need—they were within minutes of learning the truth.

"We've got to watch out for some kind of sign or message," Jan said. "I suppose the most likely place to look would be around the ship itself." He tried to quell the pounding of his heart as Petra and he moved cautiously out of the tree cover and walked in the direction of the spaceship. Lightning still flickered on all sides to the accompaniment of rolling thunder, sporadically illuminating the huge craft with violet-tinged brilliance.

"It's just like the other one," Petra said in a low voice as her eyes took in the fact that the ship had been subjected to incredible bolts of energy which had torn plates out of its pressure skin in some places and had melted the tough alloy in others. "It's even worse!"

Jan nodded. "There's a hell of a mess on the ground, as well. I didn't think it would be as bad as this."

In the area around the ship the scene was similar to the one they had seen earlier, except that in place of derelict earth-moving plant there was abandoned military equipment.

Tanks, bridge-layers, personnel carriers, helicopters, field guns, jeeps . . .

The tanks had been fitted with wire-guided missiles in the hope that they would be less prone to electromagnetic interference than radio-guided missiles. Almost all of the missiles had been fired and their guidance wires trailed limply from the inert tanks. Some machines were lying on their sides and others had been overturned, like toys which had been broken and scattered by a child in a tantrum.

The awesome destruction was, if anything, more complete than at the terraforming site. Two years earlier *something* had swept through the encampment with the force of a thousand tornadoes, laying waste all around it. And whatever it had been had come in fast, without warning, taking everybody off guard.

Jan and Petra knew that for sure—from the evidence of the skeletons.

They were everywhere the young couple looked—some still leaning over the controls of vehicles, some mangled by caterpillar treads. Others were lying in the open, with bony fingers still clutching laser rifles, as though they had been looking in vain for a tangible enemy against whom they could try to direct their fire.

As he walked with Petra through the scene of carnage Jan felt a bleak despair growing inside him. Until that moment he had nurtured the conviction that his brother was still alive. Bari had always been quick-witted and tough and very resourceful. Somehow, Jan had assured himself, Bari would have found a way to reach safety, no matter what forces were ranged against him, no matter how many others had died—but the shadow-eyed skulls mutely told a different story. Their message was that the Killer Planet had been too fast and too powerful, that no human being could have left this battlefield alive.

Leaden-footed, numb with grief, Jan stumbled to a halt and slumped down on a block of vine-covered masonry. Petra, seeing that Jan had at last accepted the truth, kept her distance for the moment, discreetly giving him time to recover from the initial shock.

Jan's eyes prickled painfully as he surveyed the desolation all around. A well-armed military expedition had been wiped out on this spot, and many centuries before that the population of a huge city had been annihilated by the same agency—the malignant power of the Killer Planet. He could not understand the forces which prevailed on this stygian world, nor could he hope to combat them in any way, so the only course open to him was to return to Earth as quickly as possible and try to pick up the threads of his disrupted life.

Petra came to stand by his side. "I'm so sorry, Jan," she said, sensing what he was going through.

"Poor Bari . . ." Jan's voice failed, choked off by the lump in his throat, and he hid his face in his hands, unwilling to let Petra see how close he was to breaking down. "If only I didn't feel so helpless. My brother was murdered here . . . and there's nothing . . . absolutely *nothing* I can do . . ."

Jan broke off as he saw a horrified expression appear on Petra's face. "Petra! What is it?"

"Over there!" she cried. "*Look!*"

Jan turned to follow the direction she was indicating and instantly stiffened with shock—a battle tank only fifty paces away from them had begun to move.

Jan and Petra leapt to their feet and, instinctively reacting as though the tank were under the control of a human driver, darted into the cover provided by a broken stone column. But the sentient war machine was not deceived. With an ear-splitting screech from its rusted metal tracks, it lurched forward and came directly at them, crushing everything in its path. The trailing grasses, creepers and missile guidance wires which blurred its outline gave it something of the appearance of a prehistoric mammoth.

"Oh no!" Jan breathed. "We'd better get out of here!"

"I've already gone!" Petra, sprinting as fast as she could, led the way out of the lee of the protective column before it could be toppled on them. Jan came close behind her as they ran for the cover of the jungle.

There was a nightmarish familiarity about what was happening, except that this time the conditions were worse. They had been quite tired before the deadly chase began and were unable to match their earlier turn of speed, and it would be expecting too much of their luck for another underground cavity to appear just where they needed it. The only point in their favour was that they were closer to the edge of the jungle than before, and even a battle tank powered by all the demons of hell would be repelled by that wall of massive trees.

Striving to keep up with Petra, Jan shouted, "I think we're doing better . . . this time. I think we're . . . too fast for the . . . the . . ."

"Save your breath," Petra advised. "We're not in the clear yet."

The tank churned and clanked close behind them, its corroded components emitting shrieks of mechanical fury. Fear drove them onwards. Running on adrenalin boost, they could hardly feel their feet touching the ground. They did not dare risk a backwards glance, but it was becoming obvious to them that they were outpacing the tank. They reached a flat mossy square which was bounded by the jungle on its far side, and were sprinting across it— only seconds away from safety—when the unthinkable happened.

A second tank burst through the wall of a ruined building ahead of them, barring their escape route.

Petra, who was still slightly in the lead, slid to a halt, her thoughts in chaos. The first tank was howling and thundering close behind them, threatening to crush them at any second. She swung to the left and ran parallel to the jungle's edge, with Jan on her heels. From behind them came an ear-punishing squeal of metal tracks as both tanks came in pursuit.

They tried to increase speed, but the dreamlike adrenalin flight was no longer possible for them. They were breathing in noisy rasps, and their limbs felt as though they were made of lead. Their feet were slapping loudly on the pavement, a sign that they were both nearing total exhaustion. They were on the verge of collapse, whereas the huge war machines—propelled by some devilish concentration of energy—were maintaining their relentless speed. There seemed to be a note of exultation in the harsh chorus of their gear trains.

With Petra still in the lead, the pair broke through a stand of tall grass, knees sagging at every step, and saw ahead of them a rocky knoll, on top of which was what appeared to be the ruins of a temple. The knoll was surrounded by a water-filled channel which was spanned at one point by a slender marble bridge.

"Across the bridge," Petra gasped.

They ran towards the bridge, using up the last dregs of their strength, and reached it with the thundering tanks barely ten paces behind. They threw themselves on to the bridge, grabbing its balustrade for support, and by sheer force of will dragged themselves towards the safety of the far side.

The two speeding tanks converged blindly on the bridge and collided with an appalling crash of armour. The impact sent one of them off course. It narrowly missed the bridge and plunged down into the channel, sending curving sheets of water flying in all directions before it disappeared beneath the surface. Simultaneously, the other tank made a slewing correction to its course and came pounding on to the bridge.

Jan, who still had not reached the knoll, felt the marble structure heave violently beneath his feet. There was a piercing *crack* as the fragile stone beams snapped. He dived forward and grasped some trailing vines as the bridge dropped away from under him, taking the pursuing tank with it.

He clung desperately to the vines as an upflung wave of water smashed over him and seethed back into the moat, then he felt Petra's strong hands helping him to drag himself up on to the solid rock of the knoll.

"Hold on," she urged. "You're almost there."

Jan was unable to reply because he had inadvertently swallowed some brackish water, but within seconds of reaching dry land he was able to sit up and take stock of the situation. There was no trace of the death-dealing war machines except for clashing ripples in the turgid water, and the struggling shapes of wounded fish. Although it could hardly have been intended as such, the moat which surrounded the knoll had served as a perfect tank trap.

"We were lucky again," Jan finally managed to say.

Petra gave him an appraising stare, wondering if he had yet fully accepted that his brother was dead. "Yes, but how long can that kind of luck hold out?"

"Not much longer," Jan admitted. "Perhaps we've had our full ration already."

"That's what I was thinking." Petra was sitting cross-legged on the ground, breathing heavily as she recovered from the second dreadful chase, and Jan could see that for the first time her composure was beginning to crack. She was trembling slightly and her face bore a hunted expression, the blue eyes dulled with weariness and apprehension.

"In that case . . ." Jan paused, swallowing painfully. His grief over the loss of his brother was returning in full spate now that the immediate threat to their lives had been lifted, but at least he had been freed from the heavy load of obligation which had burdened him for years.

"In that case," he said more firmly, "the sensible thing to do would be to head back to the *Seeker* and blast off for home."

Chapter 7

The decision to abandon the mission having been made, they scanned the surrounding plain, taking advantage of the slight elevation they had attained, checking for any sign of movement in the scattered military equipment. All was quiet for the moment, as though the mysterious force which could propel tanks without help from their engines, had expended its fury for the time being. The only semblance of life came from the lightning which stalked the horizons, growling in the insubstantial throat of the atmosphere.

They knew they should get back to the rocket ship without delay and leave Verdia behind as quickly as possible, but they were now desperately tired and in need of an interlude in which to regain their strength.

"How do you feel about resting for a few minutes before we set out?" Petra said. "I never thought I would say this, but I'm so hungry I'm even looking forward to eating some more of that awful tennis-shoe toffee."

"It would be a good idea to have a break." Jan glanced around. "But I'd feel safer if we were under cover."

Petra looked up the slope and saw a break in the wall of the circular ruin which crowned the knoll. "Let's try up there—we might be able to get into the old building."

They stood up and climbed slowly to the gap in the wall. The space beyond was largely taken up by collapsed walls and roof beams, but they could see an opening to a small chamber which had remained more-or-less intact. They unslung their bows, squeezed their way into the chamber and flopped down in the near-darkness with sighs of relief.

The watery grey radiance which managed to penetrate down through the clouds was too weak to illuminate the interior of the chamber to any great extent, but they did not mind. It was purely psychological, they knew, but they felt more secure in the near-darkness, as might hunted animals sheltering in a burrow.

They had come a long way since they had brashly undertaken to conquer the Killer Planet.

"I think we'll be all right here for a while," Jan said. "You know, it seems ages since we had that drop of champagne in the office—but it was only this morning. So much has happened."

"*Too* much, if you ask me."

"Yes, but at least we're going back now. Just think! If we make good progress back to the *Seeker*—and get picked up quickly when we get into orbit—we might even be back in Jacksonville by nightfall on the same day. That's if the quarantine police don't lock us up for too long."

"They'd better not try it," Petra said. "I've got things to do at home."

"Yeah, and I need to tell Dad about Bari as soon as possible. He's entitled to know, to have his mind put at rest. Once that's been done I might feel as though I had achieved something—little though it is."

"You have achieved a *lot*, Jan." Petra was silent for a moment. "I'm only sorry you had to find out at last that your brother is . . ."

"Dead," he supplied for her. "You don't need to avoid the word—I'm getting over the first shock of it now and I'm starting to get reconciled to the idea. In an odd way, I think I have always known the truth—somewhere deep down inside me—but I couldn't admit it to myself. Perhaps Dad was the same. Your mind can behave strangely. This way, knowing that Bari is at peace, we can all be at peace . . . eventually . . ."

Jan's voice broke with emotion and suddenly, there in the darkness of the ruined alien temple, the tears he had held back earlier were coursing down his cheeks. He felt Petra's arm steal around him and he buried his face in her shoulder as bitter sobs racked his body. After a while the act of expressing grief, and the simple comfort of human contact, did their healing work and he sat up feeling emotionally wrung-out but strangely relieved. The inner warfare between his subconscious and conscious mind had ceased, and there was a blessed quietude at the core of his being.

"I'm all right now," he said. "And once we've got some nourishment inside us I'll race you back to the *Seeker*. Okay?"

"You've got yourself a deal," Petra said as she opened the supplies pouch attached to her belt. Making herself as comfortable as she could, she brought out a bar of the food concentrate and began to chew it.

"This stuff isn't all that bad, you know." Jan made some appreciative noises. "The taste isn't too exciting, I admit, but what we have here is a scientifically proportioned blend of essential ingredients—just what we need to keep us going."

"Yes, but it shouldn't be beyond the powers of 22nd Century science to make it taste half-way edible," Petra replied. Her eyes were adapting themselves to the dimness, picking out more and more detail in the surroundings, and it was when starting on the second bite of her food bar that she turned her head to the right and made an unnerving discovery.

They were sharing the tiny chamber with a human skeleton.

Petra stopped chewing, instinctively flinching away from the grisly object which was slumped against the wall not far from her, on the side farthest from Jan.

"What's wrong?" Jan whispered, aware of her reaction.

She made her voice calm. "There's nothing to worry about—we're in no danger—but there's a skeleton of a man over to my right."

"What?!" Jan began to scramble away towards the entrance of the chamber, but Petra gripped his arm and held it until he relaxed again.

"Take it easy," she said. "Skeletons are the least of our worries."

"Sorry—my nerves are still on edge." Jan settled down again, unable to move his gaze away from the barely-seen figure, and in an effort to compensate for his jumpiness fixed his eyes on a glint of metal near the skeleton's neck. "I can see his identification tag—perhaps we should bring it back with us."

"Suit yourself."

"I'll do it." In spite of all the carnage and destruction he had witnessed during the course of the day, Jan was far from inured to death, and he had difficulty in overcoming his natural revulsion as he moved closer to the skeleton. He studied the crumpled form and made out the tattered remains of an SEF officer's uniform. It appeared that the man had taken refuge in the ruin when the machines went on their deadly rampage, and perhaps had died of starvation.

Verdia's teeming insect life would have done the rest. Feeling like an intruder in a tomb, Jan abandoned the idea of collecting identification. He turned to crawl away, and as he did so the tip of his sword brushed against the bony remains.

"My name is Major Dorey Haines," the skeleton said, "and I am a senior science officer with the . . ."

The rest of the sentence was lost to Jan as he began a feverish scramble towards the entrance of the chamber, to get away from the terrifying apparition. Then his common-sense reasserted itself. There had been a hissing sharpness to the voice which indicated that it was coming from a micro-recorder. Shamefaced, he turned back to the skeleton, and this time he noticed the microrecorder bracelet on one of the fleshless wrists. The dead officer must have made a record-ing for the benefit of posterity and set the machine to play automatically at the slightest touch.

"That scared the hell out of me," Jan confessed to Petra, who had not moved. "I didn't expect a voice to come out of a . . ."

"Listen to what it's saying," Petra cut in. "It might be important."

" . . . have been here at this landing site for only two hours," the recorded voice went on, an echo from two years in the past, "but already there are signs that something very strange is taking place. There is a huge build-up of electrical potential in the area. One can see the Saint Elmo's fire shining around the tips of antennae and masts, and I have noticed glowing fingers of it reaching down from the clouds in many places. The signs are that we are going to have a very severe electrical storm.

"My instruments show that there is a powerful flow of electromagnetic force streaming into the camp. It seems to originate at the planet's north pole, which is only about two kilometres from here. Visibility is poor, but the radarscope shows that there is a peculiarly shaped tower at the precise position of the pole and it appears to have, somehow, escaped the destruction which laid low the city which once occupied the rest of this area.

"That is something I plan to investigate at the earliest possible moment, but my main priority at present is to contact Colonel Tout and persuade him that we should disperse our people and equipment as quickly as . . ."

At that point the recorded voice was lost in a fierce crackling sound which was followed by a period of silence.

"That was probably the beginning of the attack," Jan said, stirring out of his chilled fascination.

"It sounded that way." Petra felt a pang of sadness. "I wonder if . . ." She stopped speaking as another burst of crackling came from the recorder and the voice from the past was heard again. This time it was weak and barely recognisable, the well-constructed sentences having given way to disjointed phrases.

". . . terrible . . . *terrible* . . . never seen anything like it . . . machines have a life of their own . . . missiles firing by themselves . . . everybody dead . . . bodies crushed . . ."

There was another silence, and when the voice resumed it was calmer than before but very faint, as if the speaker was being overcome by a deadly weariness.

"I hoped I would have been safe once I had crossed the bridge to this old temple, but I took a bullet or a piece of shrapnel in the back. It's all quiet out there now. Oddly enough, I can't feel any pain. I don't know if that's a good sign or a bad one.

"I don't know how much time I have left . . . and I don't even know if this recording will ever be heard by another human being . . . but in the hours I have been lying here I have reached some conclusions about what happened out there . . .

"It may sound as though I'm delirious, but I believe there is a malign intelligence at work on this planet, one which orchestrated the destruction of our expeditions.

"I also believe it is an *alien* intelligence. Alien to this world, that is. The ancient Verdians had a flourishing civilisation here, and it didn't simply crumble away. It was destroyed suddenly . . . in the same way that we were destroyed . . .

"I believe that an alien creature arrived here from space many hundreds of years ago. It has a blind hatred for all other forms of intelligent life. It also has the power to control and direct electromagnetic forces . . . a power which enables it to take control of any metallic machine and turn it against its operators . . .

"I believe that the alien being is still alive . . . in the tower which marks Verdia's north pole . . . and it is feeding on . . . feeding on . . .

"It's getting very dark in here. Why is it getting so . . . ?"

Jan and Petra bowed their heads as silence descended on the chamber. There had been a finality about the last whispered words which told them the recording had ended—for ever.

At length Petra said, "Another five minutes or so, Jan—then we should get out of here."

Jan raised his head and scowled into the darkness, forgetting about his need to eat. "You know, what we just heard sounded crazy. I doubt if anybody back home would ever credit it, but *we* know that everything Major Haines said was right. The machines don't simply go wild—they act as though they're being guided by . . . how would you put it? Some kind of evil intelligence."

"That's right," Petra agreed. "They were definitely *hunting* us—that's why we want to get away from this damned mudball of a world as soon as possible."

"Yes, but what's sticking in my gullet is the major's explanation, this idea about an alien coming down out of space a long time ago. Who's to say it isn't true? We've only explored a small fraction of the galaxy, and it's quite possible that out there somewhere are creatures who can control some natural forces and use them to kill anybody they see as an enemy."

"And you think there's one of them right here on Verdia," Petra said. "In that tower at the north pole?"

"The more I think about it the more certain I am." Jan clenched his fists as fury boiled through his mind, driving out his former fatalistic acceptance of his brother's death. "Bari and all the others were murdered by some kind of *thing*. It's only a couple of kilometres away—skulking in that tower—and there's nothing we can do about it. It's too powerful. It can turn back an army attack. In fact, the better equipped any force which went against it, the more certain it would be of winning—because there would be more weapons to turn against the attackers."

Listening to Jan's words, Petra felt a cool tingling along her spine as a strange idea took shape in her mind. *Could the alien's strength also be its weakness? Could those very attributes which made it so all-powerful also contain the seeds of its defeat?*

"What if somebody attacked the monster *without* any

weapons?" she said thoughtfully, almost as if musing aloud.

Jan snorted. "I can think of much better ways to commit suicide."

"I don't mean with no weapons at all. I mean with weapons that the monster wouldn't be aware of . . . wouldn't be able to control . . . like our swords and bows. That's why they were made of plastic in the first place, isn't it?"

"My *God!*" Jan went rigid with excitement. "You're absolutely right! Just think—if we could approach the tower undetected, and get inside it with our swords, we'd be a bigger threat to the monster than an entire army equipped with modern weapons!"

Jan fell silent for a moment as he explored the new idea and its implications. It was ironic to think of man's simplest and most basic weapon, hardly changed since the days of the Roman empire, being more effective than a full squadron of battle tanks or warplanes. His heart began a steady and powerful pounding as he considered putting the plan into action. Everything seemed quiet on the plain surrounding their refuge on the rocky knoll. If the alien was making the mistake of presuming them dead, all they had to do was slip quietly away into the jungle and make their way to the tower.

"This changes everything, doesn't it, Jan?" Petra's voice was quiet but intense. "You know where your enemy is now—and you want to go after it."

"Yes, but . . ." Jan hesitated.

"But what?"

"It's going to be really dangerous going into that tower . . . there's a very good chance of not coming out again . . . and it was *my* brother who was killed."

Petra gave an impatient sigh. "Jan, are you trying to say that this is a personal thing? That I'm not really involved?"

"I . . . I suppose that's about it."

"Well, think again," Petra said firmly. "How many innocent people has that beast killed? Hundreds of humans; perhaps millions of Verdians. No, Jan, this isn't a personal matter—it's an all-out war between that monster and the entire human race. *Both* of us happen to be in the front line, and *both* of us are taking the enemy on."

Jan nodded gratefully. "Thanks, Petra. I guess I . . ." He broke off as—abruptly—the stillness outside the ruin was shattered by the clanking of armour and machinery.

The two friends crawled rapidly out of the makeshift hideout, half-rose to their feet and peered over the ruin's perimeter wall. The scene which met their eyes caused them to step back from the wall, dry-mouthed with dread.

A military bridge-laying machine was in the process of spanning the moat with massive steel girders, and beyond it several tanks were already rolling forward, ready to surge on to the knoll as soon as the way had been prepared.

The death hunt was on again!

Chapter 8

Side by side, they climbed the low wall and dropped down to the path which ran around the perimeter of the ruined building. It may have been a trick of the imagination, but it seemed that the mechanical uproar from the war machines had increased as soon as they came into the open.

"Perhaps there's another bridge at the opposite side of the hill." Petra kept her voice firm, giving no indication of the fresh fears that had begun to seethe within her.

"Let's see!"

As they sprinted to the other side of the knoll it became apparent that the noise from the lumbering machines actually was louder and more insistent. The implication was that the alien being, in spite of being two kilometres away, knew exactly where its human adversaries were at any given moment and was able to direct its mechanical slaves to them.

"The monster knows where we are," Petra said. "I wonder how it does that."

"All I can think of is that it must be some kind of electrical trick," Jan breathed, struggling to keep pace with Petra on the narrow path. "The alien's nervous system might act a bit like a radar set, spreading some kind of electrical field out for kilometres on all sides."

"I see! Our brains work with electrical impulses, don't they? That could cause a local disturbance in the alien's own field, letting it pinpoint where we are at any . . ." Petra broke off as they stumbled to a halt at the rear of the knoll, their hopes of finding another bridge abruptly shattered. The moat's implacable dark waters barred their way.

A thunderous booming vibration was suddenly added to the sounds coming from behind them, and they knew only too well what it meant. The military bridge had been completed and the tanks had already begun to cross it.

"We'll have to swim for it," Jan said tersely.

"That's what I was thinking," Petra replied. "Are you ready?"

"Ready!"

Aware that they had only seconds in hand, they scrambled down the steep slope towards the moat. Jan was slightly in the lead as they reached the edge. He took a deep breath in preparation for the two-metre dive into the water, and had actually begun the forward plunge when he saw something which contorted his face with dread.

The water of the moat was alive with glistening black shapes which were cruising like sharks just below the surface.

"The fish!" Petra cried. "Watch out for the . . ."

Jan pulled back, fighting to retain his balance, but his feet slipped on the slimy rock. As he fell he twisted in the air and grabbed with both hands at the vines which seemed to grow everywhere on Verdia. His fingers clamped on the ropy foliage, which perversely tore away from the rock, but by then Petra had leaned down and gripped one of his wrists, checking his descent. He found a foothold and was able to work his way on to a ledge just above the water.

He signalled for Petra to join him and she immediately

76

lowered herself over the stony edge. Bodies taut with urgency, they looked down and Petra got her first look at the hideous denizens of the moat. This close to the water they could see more detail of the creatures which swarmed just below the surface. They were black, several metres in length, and seemed to combine the attributes of shark and squid—torpedo-shaped forebodies terminating in clusters of tentacles. As Jan and Petra gazed down at the creatures with repugnance, one of them momentarily opened its mouth to reveal rows of jagged teeth. The sight left no doubt at all that a plunge into the murky waters of the moat would mean near-instantaneous death.

"Ugh!" Petra shuddered in revulsion. "We'll have to forget about swimming."

"I know," Jan replied, trying not to show his despair. "But we have to do *something*—and soon!"

The ledge on which they were perched began to vibrate and a few pebbles bounced down past them, dislodged from the path above. At least one tank was nearing their position, and all it had to do was blunder down the slope above them to bring their lives to a sudden and very violent conclusion.

Is this really the end? Petra thought, her mind chilled with fear. *Are we about to be crushed by a driverless tank, or become food for a pack of . . . ?*

"Food!" she cried out. "That's it—*food!*"

Jan stared at her in bafflement.

"Look how many of the horrors are packed into the moat. It can't possibly provide enough food for them—so they must be cannibals!"

"What does . . .?" Jan's brow cleared. "If we cut some of them . . . start them eating each other . . . it might distract them enough to let us swim across."

77

"It's our only hope."

Moving with controlled urgency, aware of the rock face trembling with the weight of the approaching tank, Jan and Petra unsheathed their swords and stabbed down at one of the cruising black shapes. The incredibly sharp plastic blades sliced into the dark flesh, releasing swirls of inky fluid.

The result was immediate, dramatic and appalling.

Almost before they were able to withdraw their swords there was a convergent surge of glistening black bodies which completely overwhelmed the wounded creature. Within a few seconds it had disappeared, torn apart by dozens of its fellows, some of which—in a primal frenzy of blood lust—blindly attacked each other. Hundreds of others, drawn by the scent of food, swarmed into the area with incredible speed, turning the surface of the moat into a heaving, threshing mass of scaly bodies and tentacles.

Jan and Petra knew at once that there was no hope of swimming across the moat. They glanced at each other, wide-eyed, as the same desperate idea was born in their minds. In that instant of near-telepathic communion, both knew exactly what had to be done, and they rose to their feet as the menacing shape of a tank blotted out the light from above them. Not daring to think about what might happen, they launched themselves out from the rocky ledge—on to the living surface.

With three superhuman, fear-boosted strides—moving in perfect unison—they crossed the moat and gained the opposite bank. Jaws snapped loudly at their heels.

Reaching firm ground, driven by all the forces of nightmare, they ran for the jungle without looking back. Behind them there was a sliding rumble followed by a crash, and Jan knew the tank had careered down into the moat.

"That's the third time we've been lucky," he said, feeling thankful simply to be alive.

Petra shot him a sideways glance. "Yes, but there has to be a limit . . ."

As if to confirm her words, the pattern of events changed immediately. On previous occasions when one of the pursuing machines had been put out of action there had been a blessed lull in the activity, as though the effort of propelling the juggernaut by remote control had tired the malign alien. This time, however, they were not to be granted a breathing space. As they neared the wall of trees and foliage the mechanical screeching behind them abruptly increased in volume, going into a crescendo. The shrieking of rusted metal wheels and tracks, forced into motion for the first time in two years, made the air hideous.

Jan and Petra glanced back and their spirits quailed when they saw that every intact war machine and vehicle in the cleared area was stirring into life.

It was obvious that the alien monster was going all out for the kill!

With the clamour of the pursuing armour ringing in their ears, they reached the edge of the jungle and plunged into it. Before they had covered more than a few metres they were forced to use their swords to hack a path through tough undergrowth. They consoled themselves with the thought that the jungle was a natural barrier which was helping to save their lives. It was possible for them to slip in between the closely spaced tree trunks, whereas the bulky vehicles were forced to make detours.

As Petra was hacking at a barrier of tough vines it

occurred to her that the tanks might be able to do the same thing on a vastly larger scale with their weapons. She put the idea to Jan and was relieved when he shook his head.

"The tanks' laser cannon and flame throwers would have been able to blast a path through the jungle if they had been in working order," he said. "But two years of rain and rust are bound to have put them out of action."

That was one factor in their favour, they knew, but was it enough to enable them to negotiate safely the two horrendously difficult kilometres to the planet's north pole?

As they struggled to cut their way step by step through the impeding masses of foliage, Jan was forced to admit to himself that he was rapidly running out of strength. He glanced at Petra. Her hair had straggled down from under her jungle hat and, though she was keeping up the pace and wielding her sword as effectively as any man, her face was taut with weariness and strain. She had displayed boundless courage and loyalty—and he knew she was prepared to go with him into the alien's lair itself—but their growing exhaustion was a major cause for concern . . .

Jan ceased his battle against the resilient vegetation, and on seeing him pause Petra did likewise.

"Are you all right?" she said, taking deep draughts of the humid air.

He shook his head, chest heaving as he laboured for breath. "I'm having second thoughts. This is killing us. Even if we manage to reach the tower that Major Haines talked about, we're bound to be on the point of exhaustion—and the tanks might still be on our trail."

"We can't let the monster get away with everything it has done."

"No, but I'm beginning to think that the sensible thing to

do—and also the surest way to finish the monster off —would be for us to head back to the *Seeker* and get away from this hellhole. As soon as we get into orbit we're bound to be picked up by a police vessel."

"That's . . ." Petra paused as an unusually fierce bolt of lightning was followed by an ear-punishing thunderclap. "That's all very well—we'd be scolded and packed off home—but what about the monster?"

Jan wiped sweat from his brow. "That's the whole point! We are the only two human beings who know of the monster's existence. But when what we have learned is passed on to the Council of Empire our armed forces will easily be able to deal with the alien. It calls all the shots when it's dealing with ground forces, but just one nuclear bomb lobbed down from orbit would blast it to hell."

"You're forgetting the Council has closed the book on this planet," Petra said. "They just aren't interested in it."

"That was when they thought they were up against the natural forces of the whole planet," Jan insisted. "But when they learn they're dealing with a single alien entity—a murderous invader—everything will be different. When they realise they can have an entire world for the cost of a single bomb they'll have a rush of patriotism to the head. That's the way those people think."

"You could be right," Petra said, tilting her head as she weighed up the idea. "There's going to be a problem in getting them to believe us, though—we should have taken Major Haines' recorder."

"Damn!" Jan slashed at a visibly moving creeper. "It's too late now—we'll just have to convince everybody by our own efforts. What do you say? Do we head back to the *Seeker*?"

"Suits me." Petra gave him a tired smile. "This is hardly my idea of a perfect day, you know."

"That's it decided then." Jan gave a sigh of relief. "We head back to the *Seeker*."

Now moving at a less tiring pace, and with a great load lifted from their minds, Jan and Petra renewed their attack on the tangled vegetation, clearing the way with smooth sweeps of their grey blades. Relying on their sense of direction, they veered their course to the south. Once they had neared the site where the development team had landed they knew they would soon be able to find their way to the *Seeker*. And within seconds of reaching the rocket ship they would be soaring up through the clouds, on their way to safety.

A few minutes after the change of course they reached a clear, shallow stream which flowed in a generally southerly direction. Mindful of how dangerous the waters of the dark moat had been, they inspected the stream carefully, but it looked as innocuous as a similar waterway on Earth.

Reassured by what they saw as a good omen, Jan stepped into the stream. "Come on in—the water's lovely."

"Very original remark," Petra said as she stepped down into the stream.

"It was the best I could do in the current circumstances," Jan replied. "Do you get it? Water . . . current . . ."

"I got it, but I didn't want it." Petra was glad to see that Jan was regaining something of his boisterous spirit, and she also enjoyed the coolness of the water as it seeped through her boots. Now that they no longer had to slash their way through dense vegetation progress was much easier and faster, but they had been following the course of the stream for only ten minutes or so when she thought she heard a disturbing sound. She stopped, frowning, and cupped a hand to her ear.

"What's the matter?" Jan said, moving closer to her.

Petra signalled for him to stop swishing his feet through the water. "Listen!"

Jan halted, straining his ears, and immediately identified the source of Petra's alarm. The sound of the tanks and other vehicles battering at the jungle's defences had been steadily fading—but now it appeared to be increasing in volume again.

Baffled by this new development, they turned their heads this way and that. An extra-loud series of crashes told them that some large trees had been brought down by sheer mechanical brute force. Birds squawked raucously in the distance as their habitats were destroyed.

A second later Jan and Petra heard the now-familiar clanking and shrieking of unlubricated machinery in motion.

"I'll try to have a look." Jan stepped out of the stream, ran to a tall yellow-leaved tree and swarmed up its trunk until he could see a considerable distance through the mist and gloom to the south.

What he saw brought a painful prickling of cold sweat to his forehead.

"Can you see anything?" Petra shouted.

Jan nodded silently, not yet trusting himself to speak. All the bulldozers and earth-movers which had belonged to the development team were ranged line abreast and were heading towards Petra and him!

"Jan!" Her voice was insistent. "Have I got to climb up there as well? What can you *see*?"

"The bulldozers . . . and all the other machines . . .

they're coming this way . . . they're battering down the trees."

"But we thought they couldn't do that."

"We were wrong," Jan said, gazing at the scene with grim fascination.

The vast machines—each weighing many thousands of tonnes—were travelling fast, driven by the fearsome alien power, and were flattening the jungle before them. Together they formed an irresistible force which nothing could halt. The continuous rank they formed barred the way back to the *Seeker*.

Lightning flickered through the murk on all sides as though trapdoors to hell were being opened, emphasising the demonic nature of the energies which were being unleashed by the juggernauts' alien overlord.

Jan worked his way down to the ground, sagged against the tree trunk and gave Petra a troubled stare. "The rotten filthy monster has us beaten. I don't see how we're going to get out of this."

"We're bound to be able . . ." Petra let the sentence tail off, aware of how hollow words of optimism would have sounded. In spite of her resilient spirit she was beginning to feel overwhelmed by the sheer magnitude of the forces opposing them.

This was yet another cruel reversal of their fortunes. Each time it had seemed that events were going to swing in their favour, a malignant Fate had stepped in and turned the tables against them. It looked to her as though they had only been given hope so that the subsequent despair would be all the greater. The difference this time was that the reversal was final. The alien adversary was making its ultimate move against them—and there was no prospect of escape.

Jan bowed his head and remained in the attitude of defeat for several seconds, unable to face a continuation of the unequal struggle—then a private miracle occurred.

Hatred—pure, cold, unadulterated hatred—came to his aid.

The alien invader lurking at Verdia's north pole might have physical superiority over any human being, but he was never going to give in to it—not *ever!*—because that would be betraying his own brother and all the others who had perished on this world. It was tragic that Petra too was almost certainly doomed—but it was beyond his power to do anything about that—and the thought of her death served only to strengthen his resolve. If he and Petra had to die anyway, they were going to die in one last act of defiance against the alien monster.

And the message to it would be: *Enjoy your triumph while you can, alien, because our kind will not tolerate your existence. Sooner or later—we will destroy you.*

Jan raised his head and saw Petra gazing at him with a peculiar, bleak-eyed intensity. Again there was a moment of near-telepathic understanding, and he knew at once that her thoughts had been running in the same direction as his.

"We've decided, haven't we?" she said in a deceptively casual voice. "We go for the kill."

Jan nodded slowly. Together they stepped into the stream and began to retrace their footsteps—heading due north.

Chapter 9

Trying to strike a balance between moving quickly and conserving their strength, Jan and Petra maintained their distance from the advancing bulldozers. The crash of falling trees from behind them mingled with the rumbling of thunder.

As they walked through the humid gloom they kept a close check on what was happening to their left. One of their principal worries was that some of the tanks might have battered their way through thinner parts of the jungle, blocking the way to the north, but there was no sign of them and nothing to be heard from that direction.

"It's almost *too* quiet up ahead," Jan said uneasily.

"The monster seems to have every confidence in the bulldozers," Petra replied. She refrained from adding that such confidence seemed justified—the line of terraforming machines which were steadily smashing their way through the trees constituted a terrifying and unstoppable force.

After some twenty minutes the stream began to meander away to the east, ceasing to be of value as a jungle pathway. Jan consulted his tiny compass.

"The needle's standing on end," he said. "It looks as though we've come as far north as we need."

Petra noticed a low place in the left bank and led the way out of the stream. The fern-covered ground sloped upwards for some distance, blocking their view to the north, but they both knew that from the top of the gradient they would be able to see the enigmatic tower which housed their enemy. The time for the final conflict had almost arrived.

Jan summoned up a humourless smile. "It looks as though this is where we go . . . What did they call it in all the old war movies? . . . over the top."

Petra returned the smile. "I always preferred comedies."

"Petra . . ." Jan hesitated. "In case we don't get another chance to talk, I'd like to say . . . What I mean is . . ."

"I already know what you mean," Petra said, keeping her voice calm, resolutely thrusting aside her natural fears. "Don't you think it would be best if we got on with the job and saved the talking till later?"

Jan nodded. "Let's go!"

They climbed the long slope and at the top had to clamber over some lichen-covered masonry, a reminder that the whole area had once been a city. Old instincts prompted them to negotiate the massive blocks as quietly as possible.

They then found their view obscured by a screen of shrubs and tall fleshy fronds, but they did not need to see the alien being to know they were close to it. The air was oppressively hot and heavy, loaded with electrical tension, and although there was no breeze Jan felt the hairs on his forearms begin to stir. They had become charged with static electricity. Without any help from scientific instruments, Jan and Petra could tell that they were close to the inconceivable concentration of power which surrounded their monstrous enemy.

"Can you hear a noise like a dynamo?" Petra said. "A kind of low humming?"

"I'm not sure if I can hear it or *feel* it." Jan pressed a fingertip against one of his ears. "And there's something else, isn't there? This is like telepathy . . . you can sense something . . . the monster is *gloating* . . ."

"It knows exactly where we are," Petra said in a low voice. "It's waiting for us."

"In that case, let's not disappoint it."

Jan and Petra tightened their grips on their swords and swung the grey blades, cleaving the screen of vegetation. They froze into shocked immobility as they took in the scene which lay beyond.

Several hundred metres away was a squat, windowless black tower—the stronghold of the inhuman fiend which had descended on Verdia centuries earlier. The force of evil and of hatred emanating from it was almost tangible, a silent assault on the mind which made all who encountered it want to cower away.

No vegetation grew in the vicinity of the tower, as though even plant life was repelled by the thing which lurked within. The ground all around was flat and paved with dark granite, looking much as it would have done when the ancient city was in its heyday, forming a perfectly level battleground.

And on that battleground, their menacing shapes fitfully illuminated by lightning flashes, were perhaps fifty tanks and other machines of war. They were slowly circling the black tower in two contra-rotating rings, forming an impenetrable defence.

"My *God!*" Petra gasped as the burden of total despair descended on her.

Standing beside her, Jan swore bitterly. The slim hope they had pinned on the possibility of primitive hand-to-hand combat with the alien had vanished. This was why there had been no attack from the military machines as he and Petra were making their way north along the bed of the stream. The alien, knowing where they were going, had summoned the armoured juggernauts directly to it—and now they were ready to destroy the insignificant humans who had dared oppose their master.

"We're finished!" Jan whispered, his eyes prickling with sheer frustration and dismay. "We're completely done for!"

"It looks . . ." Petra tilted her head. "Listen!"

From behind them came the sound of crashing trees and the squealing of machinery. The army of bulldozers and earth-movers, steadily approaching from the south, had almost caught up with them. They were trapped at the centre of a legion of invincible steel monsters!

Pale and silent, Jan and Petra exchanged glances and then—accepting that there was no hope of escape in any direction—walked forward on to the dark granite of the huge plaza. Several of the tanks circling the tower turned and surged towards them at once, their tracks emitting discordant screeches of triumph as they converged on their human quarries. A moment later, behind the pair, the last trees of the jungle were toppled and crushed as the enormous shapes of the bulldozers came into view. Petra and Jan were now almost completely surrounded by the instruments of the alien invader, and the trap was inexorably closing on them.

Jan lowered his head and tried to compose himself, wondering how quickly the end would come, and if there would be much pain. He felt oddly at peace with himself. His main regret was that Petra and he had not even been able to scratch the alien, but they could hope that others would one day follow in their footsteps, and that they would inflict on the alien the punishment it so richly deserved.

Petra, walking with her head held high, found it difficult to accept that she had entered the last minutes of her life. Death had always seemed a remote event, especially as medical science had extended life expectancy to almost a hundred years. To die at the age of sixteen was an unbelievably harsh consequence of her impulsive action in jumping into the *Seeker*'s cockpit when Jan had been knocked unconscious. *But there's no point in fretting about the past*, she told herself. *The thing to do now is to cheat the grim reaper for as long as possible—even if it's only for a matter of seconds.*

Jan's thoughts were interrupted by an insect-like fluttering in the breast pocket of his shirt. Bemused, wondering why he was bothering with such trivia while on the verge of extinction, he put his hand into the pocket. There was nothing there but the miniature compass. He brought it out and saw that the fluttering vibrations were being caused by the needle. It was standing vertically on its microscopic universal joint, quivering violently, a reminder that this spot was precisely on Verdia's north pole.

Jan stared at the needle for a moment, wondering why its antics should suddenly seem important to him, then his memory began to stir. He seemed to hear Major Haines, the dead science officer, speaking to Petra and him again . . .

". . . alien creature arrived here from space . . . power to control and direct electromagnetic forces . . . alien being is still alive . . . in the tower which marks Verdia's north pole . . . and it is feeding on . . . feeding on . . ."

Feeding!
FEEDING!

That was the key word!

Jan gasped aloud as he received a sudden insight into the nature of the alien. "Petra!"

Petra dragged her gaze away from the advancing tanks. "What is it?"

"The monster! It doesn't only control electromagnetic forces—it *feeds* on them!"

Petra scanned Jan's face, noting his obvious excitement. "Does that help us?"

"It might, it might," he exclaimed, almost running his words together in his eagerness to get them out. "That's why the monster decided to base itself here—exactly at the north pole. The force lines of Verdia's magnetic field are concentrated on this spot. They're food and drink to the monster. They keep it alive . . . supplying all its energy . . . giving it the power to . . . ."

"To control the machines!" Petra cut in, suddenly understanding Jan's excitement.

"Yes, and if only we can find a way of interrupting that flow of energy into and out of the monster we could isolate it from the tanks and bulldozers. They'd all stop moving. Then it would be something like a fair fight between us and the . . . ."

Jan broke off, his mind working with fear-induced speed as the tanks and bulldozers continued to close in on them. One way to prevent electrical energy waves from reaching the alien would be to encase it in sheet metal, but that was a task which would take weeks—whereas Petra and he needed a solution which could be carried out in minutes. It was crazy to imagine that such a solution existed, and yet . . . and yet . . .

"Faraday!" he half-shouted. "Faraday's Cage!"

Petra narrowed her eyes at him. "Faraday's Cage?"

"Yes, yes! You remember it from elementary physics, don't you?"

"I always found physics a bore, but wasn't it something about screening out radio waves with ... um ... wire mesh?"

"That's *exactly* it!" Jan sheathed his sword and was unslinging his bow as he spoke. "You can shut out energy waves with a sheet of metal, but Faraday discovered that you don't need a *solid* sheet. Wire mesh will do the trick just as well."

"I remember that much," Petra replied. "But we haven't got any mesh."

"No, but we've got the makings—there's wire lying all over the place. The guidance wires from all those missiles that were fired! If we could ..."

"Tie wires to the arrows and use them to wrap the wires all around the tower!" Petra was unslinging her own bow as she spoke. "We could *starve* the monster ... choke it to death ..."

"You've got it," Jan said. "Come on, Petra, let's go to war!"

The tanks were moving quite slowly now, as though their alien overlord felt secure in the knowledge that its victims could not escape and was prolonging its moment of triumph. Jan and Petra walked towards them, both drawing red-fletched arrows from the quivers on their backs.

When the nearest of the tanks were only a few metres away, and they could clearly see skeletal figures lolling in the turrets, Petra and he suddenly darted forward with all the speed they could muster. They passed between two tanks before the lumbering vehicles could converge to crush them.

Now they were barely a hundred paces from the tower and very close to the inner circle of machines which still cruised around it.

As they had been counting on, the ground here was crisscrossed with the fine wires which had once linked the tanks to their guided weapons, and which the blindly lumbering vehicles trailed like spider webs everywhere they went.

Petra knelt, picked up a free end of wire and quickly tied it to the end of an arrow. "You were right," she called out. "I think we've got a chance with this stuff."

"Yes, but keep an eye on those tanks—they're coming back!" Working with feverish haste, Jan tied a wire to one of his arrows and quickly drew the bow. He took aim, not at the black tower but at a point directly above it, and fired the arrow. It soared away through the gloom, and he saw the sun-bright needle of flame appear at its tail as the miniature motor ignited.

Driven by the powerful micro-rocket, the arrow passed over the tower, dragging a tangled skein of fine wires behind it. As the burdened arrow sagged in its flight and arced downwards the trailing network of wires settled over the tower. A moment later Petra's first arrow achieved the same result. They both leaped aside, narrowly escaping the tank which had thundered at them from behind. The machine slewed around to come after them again—but it seemed to Jan and Petra that its movements were already less forceful, less certain than before.

"Did you see that?" Petra shouted, giving a slightly unnatural laugh. "We're hurting the monster!"

"I think you're right."

Scarcely daring to hope that their scheme was taking

effect so soon, Jan and Petra ran a short distance while drawing fresh arrows from their quivers. Jan found another guidance wire and fired it off as before, with Petra doing the same thing in unison. This time, when the double skeins of wire settled over the tower, the effect on the surrounding army of vehicles was clearly noticeable.

The squeal of tracks and rusted components abruptly sank to a lower level. The machines were rapidly losing power, making Jan and Petra's task easier.

Encouraged by their success, they ran here and there among the now crawling juggernauts. Each time Jan found a sizeable tangle of wire he used one of his arrows to hurl it over the black tower. Other arrows, deliberately fired low by Petra, lapped their lines around the structure, tightening the net.

More expert than Jan with the bow, Petra was able to shoot faster and quickly expended all of her arrows, binding the tower with more and more layers of wire. Each time a new arrow was loosed off, the cage—the Faraday's Cage —which was being woven around the tower became more complete, forming a radiation-proof screen between the unseen alien and its mechanical slaves, depriving it of control.

Finally, the last circling tank and clanking bulldozer ground to a halt.

An eerie stillness, broken by only an occasional rumble of thunder, descended over the plaza.

Jan took a deep, quavering breath and stood facing the tower, his hand on the hilt of his sword. "We *did* it!" he said, exulting. "We caged the monster!"

"Yes." Petra sounded equally relieved. "And, to tell the truth, I wasn't at all sure it would work."

"To tell the truth, *I* wasn't all that sure, either." Jan did an exaggerated mime of wiping sweat from his brow.

"There's nothing to stop us going back to the *Seeker* and getting away from this miserable dump for ever," Petra said, then she looked closely into Jan's face. "Except that you don't want to do that, do you?"

"Oh, I *want* to do it," Jan assured her, "but I've just had an unpleasant thought. As far as we know, the monster is telepathic. If it has been reading our thoughts, it knows that our plan is to get the military to drop a nuclear bomb on this spot. What would you do if you were in the monster's place?"

"Get as far away from here as possible."

"Exactly! It's bound to be at least a day before the Council can react and get a military ship to Verdia, and by that time the monster will be far away from here. And as soon as it quits the tower, and gets outside the wires, all its powers will come back to it. We'll have achieved nothing."

Petra studied the enigmatic black tower and gave a slight shudder. "In fact, if the monster thinks logically it should already be on the way out." She dropped her bow and empty quiver to the ground, and drew her sword.

"Perhaps it doesn't want to face our swords, or . . ." A new note of grimness appeared in Jan's voice. "Perhaps it's waiting for us in the tower."

"In that case," Petra replied, managing to sound almost casual, "we go into the tower."

Jan felt an immediate surge of admiration and respect for her courage, but his reaction was to give an emphatic shake of his head. "No, Petra—*I* am going into the tower. Alone."

"We've already been through all this stuff," Petra said heatedly. "If you think . . ."

95

"I *have* been thinking," Jan cut in. "Just give me a few seconds to tell you what, and then you can decide what would be the best thing to do. All right?"

"I . . . I suppose so."

Jan spoke quickly. "Our one objective is to see to it that the monster gets destroyed—and that means that we now have to split up."

"Split up! But we agreed not to do that."

"Things are different now. *One* of us has to go into the tower, and I'm the logical choice, Petra. You're much better than I'll ever be with the bow, but I've been training with the sword for two years. I'm bound to have the better chance."

"Two of us would have an even better chance," Petra said, refusing to be put off so easily.

"Yes, but there's absolutely no guarantee that we wouldn't both be killed in there—and then the monster would be safe again. Isn't that right?" Jan was speaking with the persuasiveness of utter conviction. "That's why you've got to wait out here. And if I don't come out of the tower within ten minutes you've got to run—and I mean *run*—back to the *Seeker*.

"You'll have to go fast, because if the alien defeats me it is bound to leave the tower and get all the machines going again. And when you get to the *Seeker* jump into it and blast off. You have flown a light aircraft, haven't you?"

Petra nodded. "I've done about twenty hours or so in the family Cessna."

"That's good. The *Seeker* is a tricky beast to land, but all you'll have to do is go straight up. Just point her at the sky and burn your way up into space. The Quarantine Police will pick you up in no time and you can tell them everything that happened down here. Some day, if there's any justice in this universe, the authorities will get around to doing something about the monster. Doesn't that make sense?"

In spite of her instinctive feeling that it would be wrong to let Jan venture into the black tower alone, Petra had to go along with his reasoning. More important than any individual human life was the need to make public the knowledge that Verdia itself was a perfectly normal world, and that a single alien invader had been responsible for all the tragedies that had occurred beneath its leaden skies.

"I suppose you're right," she said slowly, unable to disguise her fears for Jan's safety. "But don't take any chances in there, Jan. Don't get yourself killed."

He gave a wry grimace, briefly squeezed her shoulder, then turned away and walked towards the tower. As he stepped over clumps of yellow moss, he—in preparation for the ordeal to come—banished all pretence of cool rationality from his mind and yielded to the primitive side of his nature. It was now a personal duel with the alien. The monstrous *thing* skulking in the black tower had murdered Bari Hazard and hundreds of other human beings. It had made many attempts to kill Petra and himself, and he hated it with a special, private passion which could only be satisfied in one way. The old way. It was all a question of whether or not his courage would sustain him after he had entered the dark tower to face his enemy . . .

When he was about ten paces from the black structure a door in its base—one he had not previously noticed— swung open to receive him.

He tightened his grip on the grey sword. What sort of creature was he going to find within? Would it resemble something which had crawled out from under a rock, but swollen to gigantic proportions? Or would it be so nightmarish in its alienness that nothing in his previous experience could be compared with it?

Jan's heartbeats sounded like thunder in his own ears as he reached the foot of the tower.

Carefully threading his way through the webwork of wires which shrouded the black monolith, he reached its base and paused just outside the threshold of the open door. There was total darkness inside—even the misty flashes of lightning failed to reveal any detail of what lay inside, beyond the door.

This is madness, he thought. *I'll be meeting the beast on its own ground . . . giving it every advantage . . .*

He took a tentative step forward and stood on the threshold of the black opening, then paused again, trying to force his mind into action, trying to gain some fore-knowledge of his unseen adversary.

Logically speaking, it was possible to deduce quite a lot about any creature simply by studying its environment. The complete blackness within the tower, for instance, probably meant that the creature had no eyes. Any organism which had natural radar would have no need for organs of sight.

By the same token, any creature which drew its sustenance directly from geomagnetic forces, and which could command metal objects to do its bidding, might have no need for hands. But if that were the case—how had it built the tower in the first place? Had it made use of the ancient Verdians' machines to construct its lair before it destroyed their city?

Jan did not think so. The tower was completely smooth and seamless, as though carved from one enormous block of obsidian. In fact, at close range it looked less like a building than something which had grown organically . . .

From the corner of one eye, Jan saw the door beside him give a single preliminary quiver.

My God, he screamed inwardly as the terrible truth hit him, *the tower IS the alien!*

He threw himself backwards as the door slammed like a savage mouth, its edge sending him spinning to the ground.

As he sprawled there, sick with horror and shock, he saw the edges of the door flow and disappear as it was re-absorbed into the body of the parent creature. It had been a trap specially created for him, and he had all but walked into it.

Filled with a yammering desire to put distance between himself and the monstrous being, Jan scrambled to his feet and backed away. He could sense the monster's fury and frustration—waves of hatred were telepathically battering at his mind—and suddenly he was aware of a terrible new danger.

The wires he and Petra had woven in a net around the alien were beginning to twitch and writhe.

Jan realised belatedly that the alien, having decided to lure him and perhaps Petra to their deaths, had in its cunning allowed them to think it was helpless inside the improvised Faraday's Cage. But the missile guidance wires had metal cores, and the monster could exert the telekinetic powers which remained to it on anything made of metal.

Now the wires were slithering like snakes, beginning to unwind and fall away from the alien's vast bulk. As soon as it had stripped away the radiation-proof cocoon it would again have control of its army of tanks and bulldozers. The deadly hunt would begin all over again—and this time there could be only one conclusion. The untiring metal juggernauts would not stop until their enemies were dead.

In a blind reflex of hatred, Jan dodged through the living wires, unslung his bow and reached over his shoulder to his quiver. It contained only one arrow. His face a white mask of fury and loathing, he nocked the red-fletched arrow and drew the bow.

He aimed it at the towering black hulk of the alien—then came the bleak realisation that the weapon was too puny to have any effect. A thousand such arrows would have no effect.

He lowered the bow, frantically turning his head from side to side like a cornered animal as he tried to solve the ultimate problem, to escape from the final predicament. Conventional weapons would be useless against a monster as huge and as powerful as the alien. He doubted if even a laser cannon would harm it. What was needed was sheer *power* . . . the sort of power which was unleashed by a nuclear bomb . . . the sort of power that came from the . . .

"That's it!" Jan cried aloud.

He turned on his heel and scanned the formation of tanks which enclosed the alien. Most of them had fired off their missiles during the orgy of blind destruction two years earlier, but at last he picked out one which still had a finned missle on its quadruple launcher.

Sobbing with gratitude, he sprinted to the inert vehicle and leaped up on to its sloping front end. The missile itself must have had a serious internal malfunction, otherwise it would not still be in place, but Jan's interest was not in the missile itself.

He knelt at its full reel of guidance wire, snatched out his knife and cut through the wire just behind the missile. His fingers trembling with urgency, he tied the wire to his sole remaining arrow. He stood up and drew the bow. There was no time for careful aiming, but it did not matter—for his target was the sky itself.

He released the arrow, saw the needle of brilliance flick out from its tail, then he threw the bow aside, jumped down from the tank and ran towards Petra.

"Run!" he shouted. "For Heaven's sake, *run!*"

Without wasting time on questions, she darted away, the fear he had communicated to her lending her the strength for a burst of speed Jan could not match. He could not take time for a backward glance as he bounded across the plaza, away from the dark silhouette of the alien, but in his mind's eye he saw the arrow ascending on the powerful thrust of its micro-rocket. He visualised it penetrating the low-lying cloud ceiling, the trailing wire creating a pathway for billion-volt electrical potentials . . .

The whole world seemed to explode into purple brilliance behind him.

He saw Petra throwing herself to the ground and he dropped down beside her. They huddled together on the dark granite of the plaza, unable to move as they watched the stupendous forces of nature at work. Lightning bolts struck down out of the sky, dancing and marching and counter-marching around the broken lines of tanks to the accompaniment of deafening thunderclaps.

The wire-covered alien monster, highest point in the vicinity, became a dreadful focus for unimaginably ferocious electrical discharges. Jan's and Petra's over-loaded retinas gave them a bleached-out image of frenzied lightning strikes blazing around the alien hulk, cleaving and searing and ripping its living tissue, exploding and ripping it apart. They felt the alien's telepathic death-scream—then all was silent.

The Killer Planet had lived up to its name.

Verdia had, at last, avenged itself on the alien invader which had desecrated its surface.

Chapter 10

Jan and Petra stood up, trembling in every limb. Their vision was obscured by a screen of jagged after-images caused by the lightning, and they had to blink vigorously for a moment until something like normal vision returned. When it did Petra opened her arms to him and they clung together for a reverent minute, savouring the simple joy of being alive and under no threat. The air had an after-the-storm freshness to it, making it unexpectedly good to breathe.

"I never want to go through anything like that again," Petra said in a slightly shaky voice.

"Neither do I—and we won't have to," Jan replied. "Everything's going our way now. You know, a little while ago I thought that fate had turned against us—against me, in particular—and I felt really sorry for myself, but I've just realised something. Remember how I was going to kill that black gorilla-thing when it was running away from us, and I changed my mind?"

"I remember."

"Well, just now I had only one arrow left to fire up into the clouds to trigger the lightning storm—but if I had shot the gorilla I wouldn't have had that arrow in reserve. So it looks as though luck was with us all along."

"*You* call it luck, but other people might have a different explanation," Petra said. "You gave mercy, and you received mercy in return."

"You could be right, but this is getting too metaphysical for me—and we have a couple of practical matters to deal with before we get back to the *Seeker*." Jan released Petra from his embrace and tightened his belt in a businesslike manner. "One unpleasant job, and one pleasant one."

Petra nodded, making ready to leave the scene of desolation. "What's the first job?"

"As you said earlier, we've got to go back to that temple we sheltered in and collect Major Haines' recorder. People back home are going to find it hard to believe all that went on here, and we'll need the recorder for back-up evidence."

"That's true," Petra said. "And what's the pleasant job?"

Jan was unable to repress a grin as he spoke. "We need to make some kind of a flag to plant here. The Council of Empire gave up on this world—so I'm going to claim it on behalf of the Hazard Line. You can have a chunk of it as well of course."

"You're very generous," Petra laughed. "But seriously —do you think the Council would ever recognise the claim?"

"I very much doubt it, but we're bound to get some kind of reward—enough to take care of my Dad's debts and put his business on its feet again." Jan found he was looking forward to the future with keen anticipation. "There's going to be a lot of traffic between Earth and Verdia when the development gets under way, and I'd say the Hazard Line is bound to be awarded a bunch of good contracts."

"I'm glad about that," Petra said sincerely.

"Now that I think about it," Jan went on, "it will probably be worth Dad's while to set up a permanent office on Verdia. How would you like to have a summer job here?"

Petra gave a little shiver. "I'll have to think about that."

"*I'll* be back anyway," Jan said with a note of anticipation in his voice, aware that he was entering a brand new and exciting phase of his life.

All at once, the Killer Planet had begun to seem quite a good place in which to live . . .

Mary Wesley
The Sixth Seal £3.50

Pink and green snowfalls in July are just the first in a series of
disturbing incidents worldwide – until a deadly storm blasts the life
out of everything it touches.

Only a few people remain, like Muriel, her son Paul and his friend
Henry, who are below ground when the storm strikes. Stranded in
the Devon countryside, they band together with other survivors to
make the most of their strange new world.

Inevitably, tensions rise and Henry leaves for London – and a bizarre
confrontation in the Cabinet room of 10 Downing Street. Muriel and
Paul set off in pursuit – and find themselves at the mercy of a
nightmare city . . .

Haphazard House £2.99

Haphazard House had been empty for years. A place of mystery,
damaged by fire and lost in time.

Then Lisa and her family arrive, falling for its crooked ways and
finding that the house more than lives up to its name.

Why does the village seem locked in the past? What is the secret of
the invisible gardener, and who is the eerie figure that waves from
the window of a room burnt long ago?

Robert Westall
Ghosts and Journeys £3.50

'She was running in a blind panic, out of the stock room, along the dark corridor, through the empty staff room where the kettle sang, and down the concrete stairs . . . She felt herself falling. She screamed. Then it all went black.'

When everyday things become everyone's nightmares, we move beyond the ordinary and find stories of *Ghosts and Journeys* . . .

Rachel and the Angel and other stories £3.50

'Rachel whirled in a panic. The wings were slowly opening. They might touch the altar-hangings and set them on fire! Close to tears, she ran back. And saw the most horrible thing. As the wings opened, the body began to wrinkle like skin and she knew with horrid certainty it was alive . . .'

Read on for more thrilling, mysterious and extraordinary tales.

All Pan books are available at your local bookshop or newsagent, or can be ordered direct from the publisher. Indicate the number of copies required and fill in the form below.

Send to: Pan C. S. Dept
             Macmillan Distribution Ltd
             Houndmills Basingstoke RG21 2XS
or phone: 0256 29242, quoting title, author and Credit Card number.

Please enclose a remittance* to the value of the cover price plus: £1.00 for the first book plus 50p per copy for each additional book ordered.

*Payment may be made in sterling by UK personal cheque, postal order, sterling draft or international money order, made payable to Pan Books Ltd.

Alternatively by Barclaycard/Access/Amex/Diners

Card No. | | | | | | | | | | | | | | | | | | |

Expiry Date | | | | | |

_____
                    Signature:

Applicable only in the UK and BFPO addresses

While every effort is made to keep prices low, it is sometimes necessary to increase prices at short notice. Pan Books reserve the right to show on covers and charge new retail prices which may differ from those advertised in the text or elsewhere.

NAME AND ADDRESS IN BLOCK LETTERS PLEASE:

....

Name _____

Address_____

_____

_____

_____

6/92